DEDICA

For Melanie, and for Buscemi,

CONTENTS

ACKNOWLEDGMENTS

This book was translated from *L'Ogre Amoureux* by Arthur Bernède, first published by Editions Jules Tallandier in 1929. At the time of writing, the source text is not available online.

The cover design was by Rachel Lawston of www.lawstondesign.com.

NOTE TO THE READER

Here's a new story that Chantecoq recounted to us.

We believe it will interest our readers because it takes them into a world that's somewhat unfamiliar to the general public, and because it will help them to understand, as well as the intimate morals of certain modern courts, all the secrets hidden behind the thick walls of so-called "royal" palaces.

Like all tales of the great detective, this is based entirely on reality. However we judged it necessary to change the characters' names, and to transform the country where the descendant of the sad hero of this volume still reigns, into a sort of imaginary principality.

Perhaps never has Chantecoq used more skill, more audacity, more suppleness, we'll even say more genius than in the course of this adventure.

You should have heard him narrate this truly extraordinary episode, and all with a charming modesty, a smile on his lips, in the true French style, to realise what can be achieved by the willpower of one man, armed to defend the law against a formidable power, unleashed in the pursuit of evil.

We hope that all will follow this story with the same interest that they granted to our other accounts: *The Mystery of the Blue Train*, *The Haunted House*, *The Aviator's Crime*, and *Zapata?* This story captivated us completely when Chantecoq revealed it to us himself.

Arthur Bernède

1 A MONARCH AT THE WHEEL

On April 5th 1927, a superb American car, with an interior cockpit, the most luxurious upholstery, and driven by a gentleman aged between forty and fifty years old, with a hard, authoritative gaze, a greying moustache in the American style, and a beaky nose, was driving at top speed on the road from Rambouillet to Versailles.

Next to the driver, whose elegantly refined outfit and naturally prideful and domineering attitude revealed to be a powerful man, there was another person around ten years older, his face already lined, his beard and moustache almost white, his nose slightly turned up, his small gimlet eyes sharp and intelligent, and dressed with the sobriety of an important individual.

The first was none other than Boris I, King of Sokovia, who at that time was staying incognito in Paris under the name Count Wladimir d'Esseck.

As to his companion, he was Baron Rupert de Rurick and he fulfilled, for his sovereign, the important and delicate functions of first chamberlain and personal advisor.

Boris I was one of those modern sovereigns, very modern, who leave the trouble of governing the nation over which they've been called to reign to their first ministers.

All the better for the people, especially when they're condemned to have as a head of state a prince so unfit to govern as the man whose portrait we just sketched.

Boris I, indeed, had never been destined to ascend to the throne.

He belonged to a Balkan family whose origins were lost in the annals of history.

Legend, more than history, claimed that the Markéwitches had once reigned over certain ill-defined countries located in Lower Austria, which were then independent.

The Markéwitches, whose fortune, acquired under rather unclear circumstances, had increased through the stock markets much more than over time, could therefore add to their opulence the prestige of a glory much more subject to caution.

Whatever it was, after the Great War, when the Allies decided to redraw the map of Europe, it was decided, though no one ever knew why, that Sokovia, an Austrian province, would become an autonomous principality.

There were rather lengthy discussions as to whether it should be a republic or a monarchy. Delegates from England, Italy, Belgium and all those who had kings, opted for the Republic, but France and America, who already possessed a republican regime, opted for the monarchy.

Doubtless for diplomatic reasons which, in any case, remained mysterious, it was America and France who carried the day and it was decided that Sokovia would have the good fortune, according to some, or the misfortune, according to others, of possessing a king.

But that king had to be chosen! It goes without saying

that there were numerous competitors.

The choice of the commission charged with researching, deciding, and imposing their candidate on the Sokovian people, who were only asking for peace, alighted, after enough discussion and procrastination to make Talleyrand turn in his grave[1], on Prince Boris Markéwitch, who didn't shrink from the supreme favour that the masters of Europe had granted him.

Up to then, indeed, Boris had thought only of idly spending the immense fortune he had inherited from his ancestors, which had been boosted further by the considerable dowry brought by his wife, Princess Elisabeth d'Orwitz, daughter of one of Hungary's most opulent Magyars.

He had made no attempt to put forward his candidature and was dumbfounded on learning that he had been called to ascend to this newly constituted throne.

He uttered these rather characteristic words: "I accept… after all… on the whole, kinging, it's a good career all the same. Although it's sometimes dangerous to be a guinea-pig."

Rather wisely, however, because he was far from an imbecile, Boris began by convening Sokovia's most influential men and, after having long meetings with each of them, set his choice on a Sokovian who appeared to him to be gifted with all the necessary qualities for a statesman.

He was called the Count de Mardeck.

After being special envoy to the Emperor of Austria at

---

[1] Charles-Maurice de Talleyrand-Périgord (1754-1838). *Either* one of the most skilled diplomats in European history, *or* a career traitor who betrayed the Ancien Régime, French Revolution, Napoleon *and* the Restoration in turn. Depending on who you ask. His name has become a byword for crafty diplomacy.

The Hague, he was, after the outbreak of War, named Director General of the Austrian Red Cross in Geneva.

There, he had forged very strong international connections and, as much through the goodwill that he exuded as through the dignity of his attitude and nobility of his character, he had even managed to court the good graces of several allied diplomats.

Boris, in his first act, had therefore succeeded in a masterstroke.

But he ought to have stuck with that. Indeed, with the cynicism which characterised him, as soon as he had obtained the Count de Mardeck's acceptance, he said to him, "My dear friend, I'm completely ignorant of that which they call the art of government, and I won't pretend that I have no intention of learning it. I've always been too fond of my liberty to alienate it to the profit of stuffed shirts who won't retain any gratitude for me. Therefore, you will be the true king."

"Sire," the Count de Mardeck had objected, "you're endorsing me with a terrifying responsibility."

"Why terrifying?" Boris riposted, "You're very popular in Sokovia, you've maintained excellent relations across all the regions. You'll only have to turn your hand to a few little appearances, some acts designed to inspire the public's confidence in you, and surround yourself with ministers of relative value, that's to say well-meaning, apt to take care of day to day business, and from whom you'll have nothing to fear, neither jealousies or treason, and you won't take long in becoming a great man... who will be respected, loved by everyone, and who won't be subject to any attack!"

The Count de Mardeck replied, "May I raise an objection to Your Majesty?"

"Of course, as many as you like..."

"Why wouldn't Your Majesty take on the role that he's doing the honour of conferring on me?"

"I won't beat about the bush," replied Boris. And with an almost trivial tone, he sneered, "I don't walk… because it bores me! I didn't ask to be King of Sokovia, I was sent for. I accepted because, in truth, it's not the sort of thing one refuses. But to become a statesman, to subject myself to all the administrative demands, protocols, in brief, to effectively carry out a profession for which I feel no attraction, never!

"Naturally I want to enjoy all the perks, and gather all the benefits; but I don't want to endure its tiresome aspects. All in all, these diplomatic gentlemen wanted me. I sold them my name, that's a done deal, but not my soul…

"I intend, as far as possible, to change nothing about the lifestyle I've chosen. It suits me marvellously, while you, you were born to be a minister; you have all the qualities to fulfil this role, and I'll add all the faults that it demands.

"You're perfect for it. You're one of those men who can talk for two hours without saying anything, in other words the dream orator for parliamentary assemblies. You've never been tainted by any scandal. You're rich; therefore, sheltered from all temptation. Come on, you're not going to force me to sing your praises any longer… we're agreed, aren't we?"

"Sire," replied the Count de Mardeck, "I accept. I consider I no longer have the right to refuse."

Indeed, this politician, who had managed to stay honest, understood at once that if this unfortunate country of Sokovia was to fall, in the event of his refusal, into the hands of some adventurer, upon whom Boris was perfectly capable of calling, it would lead to revolution, a new flashpoint igniting at the heart of Europe, when peace was more necessary than ever to heal wounds… and what wounds!… from which the belligerent nations were still suffering so cruelly.

Boris was much too delighted by the response the Count de Mardeck had just given to suspect for a moment the hidden meaning behind his words.

He shook his hand effusively and said to him, "Thank you. In any case, you won't be dealing with an ingrate. All the titles, all the money, all the favours you desire for you and your friends, I'm ready to grant them, because I'll never forget that you've pulled a nasty thorn from my foot."

"Sire," replied the new Prime Minister, "the best reward to which I could aspire is to be useful to my country and Your Majesty."

And so it was that the Count de Mardeck took power.

On the day of celebrations to mark the new king's coronation, carried out amid considerable crowds and remarkable splendour, if the King and the Queen, admirably beautiful beneath her diadem glittering with jewels, were gathering rapturous applause and rousing cheers, it was above all the Count de Mardeck who was the subject of endless ovations.

At once, with that marvellous instinct which guides a people, the Sokovians had guessed that their new leader wasn't the chap in the grand uniform bedecked in decorations, swaggering in a carriage and responding with an indifferent and almost disdainful air to the cheers which accompanied his passage, but the man in the black suit who was following in a second carriage, with a very simple appearance, but whose face reflected the joy of the duty to be accomplished and of the hopes that a whole nation, liberated at last, was placing in him…

Boris I was not, however, in any way jealous of the success that his prime minister enjoyed. He often congratulated himself instead, and said to himself, "Now I can relax, everything's going to turn out terribly well and I'll soon be able to resume my ordinary life."

For a while he maintained a certain decorum, which still managed to bore him deeply.

He was seen accompanying the queen, whose large clear eyes, full of sadness, seemed to give an involuntary denial to the smile that she was called upon to wear, every time that she appeared in public.

They were also seen at the theatre, at inauguration ceremonies for monuments, at exhibitions, at patriotic ceremonies which proved that a new spirit animated this country, directed by a firm and paternal hand which asked only to follow the prime minister, not his master, but his friend.

For one whole year, Boris I appeared to carry out his duties as a monarch correctly. He even threw wonderful receptions in the temporary palace where he had installed himself; because, profiting from his brand new parliament's enthusiasm, he managed to obtain the necessary credit to build an edifice worthy of his ambition.

But, after those twelve months which hadn't demanded any great intellectual effort from him, any more than they presented him with the slightest disagreement, the reveller, the hardened party animal that was the Markéwitch descendant, felt reawakening in him all the appetites that he had been obliged to rein in.

Brusquely, one day, following a royal audience over which he had presided with an ill-auguring sullen air, he asked his prime minister to stay behind and said to him brutally, in that familiar tone that he adopted in his private life, "Excellency, I've had enough. It's been a year now that I've been playing the puppet. If it doesn't stop soon, I've had enough of it!"

He could have added, as Mistinguett[2] sang, of whom he was a fervent admirer, "I'm fed up!"

But he didn't quite dare to use that slang before a statesman who, despite everything, managed to inspire a certain respect in him.

The Count de Mardeck replied, without revealing the indignation and anger that such an attitude provoked in him. "Am I to understand that Your Majesty wishes to travel…"

"By Jove!" retorted Boris. "As you put it, My Majesty needs a change of air…"

"Your Majesty," insisted the Count de Mardeck in a deferential tone, "could perhaps take within his kingdom a trip which could only add further to the devotion that his people have for him."

Boris gave an ironic sneer. "My people," he said, "couldn't care less about me, just as I couldn't care less about them. They only know you. They only swear by you."

"Have I offended Your Majesty?"

"Not at all! In fact I'm delighted, overjoyed! It's what I wanted! Here you are now almost a dictator, that was my absolute aim. In parliament, opposition is as good as non-existent, and never yet has any country practised the sacred union as well as Sokovia.

"Truly, I have nothing more to do here, other than, from time to time, to appear when you deem it useful, but not too often. Anyway, the Queen is beloved, she's very good! I'll even say that she's mad with generosity. Her entire private income is given away in alms.

---

[2] Mistinguett, aka Jeanne Florentine Bourgeois (1875-1956). Singer and actor. At one point she was the highest paid female entertainer in the world, and in 1919 she insured her legs for 500,000 Francs. As well as being a star of the silent film era, she was a regular performer at venues including the Moulin Rouge.

"She's the opposite of me, who hates mob rule, she still feels drawn to the little people. Some time ago, she paid a visit to a family who, it appeared, were plunged into misery, and she brought us back some fleas! If that amuses her, that's her business; but as for me, I have a deep revulsion for that type of insect.

"In other words, the Queen, enjoying herself here, will stay in the palace or in our Summer residence, and if the Sokovians don't have their whole king, they'll at least have half of him!"

The prime minister understood that he would be wasting his time in trying to appeal to his king's finer feelings and, above all, to his under-developed sense of duty.

He replied, hiding the sorrow that the monarch caused him. "Sire, I can only bow to your will."

"Very well! My will," cried Boris I at once, "is to go and have a nice holiday in Paris."

The Count de Mardeck declared, "I received a diplomatic message announcing that the President of the Republic intends to invite Your Majesty, and the Queen, to come to France."

"An official trip, yes, I see that…" mumbled Boris I in an ill-humoured tone. And he continued. "Oh! What's he thinking, the President of the French Republic? Couldn't he leave me alone? Am I inviting him? No, ah well! May he leave me in peace, that's all I'm asking…"

"Sire, for grave diplomatic reasons…"

"Oh! I don't even want to hear those!"

"The attachment I've pledged to Your Majesty forces me to communicate them to you…"

"I'm feeling unwell," sneered King Boris.

"Sire, I beg you, grant me five minutes. We need a great

deal of money, if we are to restore our finances and give our nation a commercial and industrial boom which will assure its prosperity."

"A while ago, I negotiated a loan with the French government. Those negotiations were better than along the right lines. I may say, with confidence, that they're almost accomplished.

"To seal the agreement, it is however vital that Your Majesty pays a visit to the President, it's the *sine qua non* agreement that the French cabinet attaches to the loan's authorisation."

"They're extraordinary, those republicans," said Boris, with a disdainful scowl. "They have no king of their own, so they must ceaselessly summon other people's. To hell with them! I'm no export commodity, and not to be exploited. If I go to Paris, and I'll go there soon enough, it will be incognito, so I can take joyful revenge for the rather morose year that I've just spent."

"Then, sire," declared the prime minister, "the project is sunk."

"No, you're intelligent enough and skillful enough to convey to the French government that this masquerade is completely pointless."

"That's not their opinion, sire, nor mine. Anyway, I'll permit myself to remind Your Majesty that he owes his crown to them."

"My crown! Did I ask them for it? They're incredible! So, they imagine I'll obey all their whims, all their fantasies, and that I'll parade through Paris like the queen of queens on mid-Lent Sunday?"

"Sire, in the name of your people…"

"My people… oh! Them! I already told you what I think

of them."

"In your own interest, sire…"

Making use of the ultimate argument that he was keeping in reserve, the Count de Mardeck intoned, "If the loan is not authorised by the French, I'll find myself in the deeply regrettable position of being forced to delay work on the palace being constructed for Your Majesty."

"Not possible!" said Boris with a start. "Oh! But then, that's another story! Why didn't you say so sooner! Damn! My dear President… you've opened up a whole new horizon that I never considered. You know what I said to you on that subject."

The statesman replied, "I do remember… Your Majesty declared to me that He would not be levied for a single centime of his personal fortune for the construction of his new residence."

"And I remain so resolved."

"Then, Your Majesty will take the decision which best suits him!"

Boris reflected for a moment, then he replied with joy. "I understand why the President of the Republic is inviting me: so that my presence provokes a wave of curiosity in Paris, which will bring a great deal of publicity to the proposed loan. That's it, isn't it, Mardeck?"

"Sire, I didn't want to say that to Your Majesty, but it is indeed the truth."

"In that case," replied the monarch, "there's no more need for hesitation: I accept the invitation. I don't want my palace to stay in mothballs. Arrange this trip in such a way that my official visit will be as brief as possible; because I intend to take the opportunity to stay in Paris incognito and taste again that wonderful lifestyle, from which I was so cruelly cut off!"

Some weeks later, the official trip took place. King Boris I and Queen Elisabeth were received as only Paris knows how to welcome sovereigns who honour the city with a visit, that's to say with courtesy, deference, and perfect tact.

The official visit, as the King of Sokovia had wished, was rather brief, but that didn't prevent him, after having sent the Queen back to Sokovia, from spending six weeks in the City of Light, where he had so much fun that he decided to buy a very fine private house, on Avenue Maillot in Neuilly, where he would come as often as possible, incognito of course, to live the life he judged ought to be his.

He kept his word.

Increasingly forsaking his kingdom, which didn't suffer, and the Queen, who was deeply affected, Boris I took ever more frequent trips to Paris, to coastal towns, in Deauville, notably, of which he was proclaimed king, which inspired a pride much greater in him than he had felt when he was named King of Sokovia.

He had to take a favourite, without giving up the repeated conquests, to which the perfect, chivalrous monarch applied himself shamelessly and successfully.

One of his former companions in debauchery, Baron Rupert de Rurick, whom he had made his friend and close counsellor, charged himself with procuring one.

She was a young Italian widow, Duchess Barbara de Castrovillari, a woman of marvellous beauty, born for intrigue, adventure, in every sense of the word, and whose husband, killed in a duel, had left her an illustrious name, but a somewhat meagre fortune.

For two years, Boris appeared rather taken with the duchess.

She benefited from this perhaps more than her conqueror had foreseen.

But once his passion had calmed, Boris wanted to be rid of her as cheaply as possible.

If he loved to enjoy himself, he could still count. Unfortunately, he found himself faced with a will superior to his own, and, as he spoke of rupture, it was enough for Barbara to whisper, quite softly, a few words in his ear before he paled and replied, "That's agreed, then, you're staying!"

And she stayed.

Closing her eyes with unheard-of complacency to her royal lover's innumerable escapades, even going, as the Marquise de Pompadour had done for Louis XV, so far as introducing him to young beauties capable of sparking desire in him, without retaining his attention for too long. Never was her influence so great as at the moment where this story begins.

Presently, she was situated near Paris, in a very fine chateau situated at the edge of the Forest of Rambouillet, the king's gift to her, where he went from time to time to pay her a visit. It was from there that he was returning, driving his car with the assurance of a professional, without a chauffeur, with, as his sole companion, Baron Rupert de Rurick, whose soul he had damned.

Boris I was an extremely sporting monarch, and he was a speed demon. That had indeed caused him a few disagreements on occasion, but no serious incidents, as he was truly a virtuoso behind the wheel.

However, everything sorted itself out easily, because he knew to compensate royally for any damage he caused.

"My dear baron," he said to his chamberlain, "how did you find the duchess?"

"Very well, still very beautiful, sire."

"The fact is she's magnificent. But didn't she seem to you to be more nervous than usual?"

"I don't think I noticed. Madame the Duchess de Castrovillari showed as always, with regard to me, an extremely flattering amiability, and I didn't notice beneath her features even the shadow of a worry, or anything that revealed an anxious mind."

Boris gave a strange smile, then he continued. "You didn't notice, then, when we arrived, the look full of lightning that she threw at me?"

"Sire, I was bowing before the duchess and, as a result, I didn't notice anything."

"Ah well! I saw it. I thought at once, the storm was about to break. Barbara is a terrible woman. She's capable of anything and although I don't have a very fine voice, she succeeded in making me sing, and it was all the better for me: I've been too weak towards her; I've let her see too clearly that I fear her. Now, she abuses it, and I fear I may never be rid of her."

"Sire," replied the Baron de Rurick, "I wouldn't want to indulge myself in any reflection which might appear to Your Majesty's eyes to be a critique of his actions."

"Rupert," cried the Count d'Esseck familiarly, "might you be on the path to your dotage?"

"Me, sire, whyever would you think that?"

"Because you're giving me the impression, at this moment, of a poor devil afflicted with complete amnesia."

"Sire, I don't understand…"

"I can see that, by Jove!"

And in ever more familiar tones, Boris, who in the world where he enjoyed himself, had been nicknamed Bobo I, cried out, "Come on, old boy, come on, to use the old French saying: don't play the ass just to make a noise. You must remember very well what I once said to you. If I nominated you as my counsellor, it wasn't for you to flatter me, fawn over me, and to break my nose with your thurible at every turn, but rather to enlighten me on my entourage's mentality and intentions, to warn me about anything which might be woven against me. In a word, to be the closest advisor of all, on whom I might entirely place my trust.

"I've put you at your ease completely; I've repeated many times that I require the whole truth from you, even should it be deeply disagreeable to me and even arouse my ill humour and anger towards you. You've not done it, Rurick."

"Sire, allow me to protest."

"Yes, yes, I know, I know... you've done great services, I acknowledge it gladly, and I believe that I've always rewarded you appropriately."

Baron Rupert affirmed, "I would be the worst of ingrates, if I didn't keep forever the memory of the benefits of every kind with which Your Majesty has blessed me."

"Then," asked the king, who had just run over a hen and hadn't even noticed, "then, why, when you saw me embarking on an intrigue with that Italian woman, didn't you cry out that it was too risky, as you'd already done in other circumstances?"

Without the slightest hesitation, the slippery fellow who was Boris's closest advisor replied in his softest voice. "Your Majesty was at that point so smitten with the duchess, that all warnings I could have offered would have been futile, and I would have incurred your disgrace, without any benefit to you, or to anyone."

"The fact is," admitted Boris I, "that I had that woman on the brain. She's a sorceress, and I would be lying if I said that at that time I considered her to be a passing conquest.

"No, I was convinced that she was going to be the woman for the rest of my life, that I had found in her the vibrant being of whom I dreamed, gifted with all the graces and destined to illuminate my life with the full force of her radiance.

"Alas! I soon realised, after having stupidly given myself over to her, after having confided in her, in moments of abandon which following momentarily satiated voluptuousness, the most important state secrets. In a word, I conducted myself like a student who had suddenly become the lover of a woman of the world.

"That's why it was impossible for me to send her away. I offered her a considerable endowment; she refused it. She said, 'I'll always be your official mistress; I'll be, all at once, your Montespan[3] and your Maintenon[4]; otherwise, I'll see to it that you lose your crown and, even worse, I'll shower you with ridicule and shame, and see you sprawling in the mud.'

"For a quiet life, I had to comply with that ragamuffin's demands. She leaves me to do just about anything I want; but even feeling such a Sword of Damocles suspended over my head is enough to poison me. You knew all that, didn't you, Rurick? Come on, won't you admit it?"

Rurick was silent.

The king, who had been forced to slow down while

---

[3] Françoise-Athénaïs de Rochechouart de Mortemart, Marquise of Montespan (1640-1707). Mistress to Louis XIV, by whom she had seven children, she wielded considerable influence at court. She was also implicated in 'The Poisons Affair', the duchess's allusion certainly carries a hint of menace.

[4] Françoise d'Aubigné, Marquise de Maintenon (1635-1719). Aka Madame Scarron, aka Madame de Maintenon. Louis XIV's second wife (married in a private ceremony and never publicly acknowledged, but generally considered to have taken place in 1683 or 1684), who at various times was friend, rival, and finally successor to Madame de Montespan in the King's affections. She wielded considerable political influence, regarded almost as prime minister in the final years of Louis XIV's reign.

crossing Saint-Cyr, cried, "You're much too crafty not to have noticed, and that's why I won't pretend I'm not angry you didn't have the frankness or the courage to talk to me about it. Because I'm convinced that, if you'd wanted to take the trouble, you could have found a way to save me from such a tiresome moral burden."

Rurick, very calm, replied, "I'll begin by begging Your Majesty's pardon, if I didn't feel I ought to warn him on this matter. Obviously, I humbly acknowledge, I lacked audacity. I also confess that I lacked clarity, and I won't hide any longer from Your Majesty that having guessed the anguish that this forced liaison was causing you, I had thought of ways to end it."

"Ah! Really!" Boris I exclaimed, as he was approaching the Porte de Versailles.

Rurick continued. "But this method, I didn't think I ought to bring it before Your Majesty."

"Why not?"

"Because you would certainly have rejected it."

"How do you know?"

"Sire, I'm so much more certain that this project, which is in the end the only practical solution, has certainly crossed your mind."

At that moment, the car was forced to slow down, because it was crossing Versailles, the town of the Great King.

Boris I, his gaze fixed ahead, remained silent, not that he was frustrated by untimely congestion; Versailles, indeed, thanks to its wide avenues and remarkably well-organised traffic control system, is one city in France where drivers can get around easily. Doubtless he was reflecting on what his confidant had just said.

The king was silent until leaving the town.

Then, as they climbed towards the steep Picardie coast, he replied, "What were we talking about just now, my dear baron?"

The baron responded, "About the Duchess de Castrovillari, sire."

"Oh, yes."

And with a wink, Boris said, "If my memory isn't playing tricks on me, you were suggesting having her poisoned, weren't you?"

"Sire, I never said that," protested the chamberlain who, now, understood all too well that he had gone too far and that he had fallen into the trap his master had set.

That master, smiling ironically, replied, "No, but you thought it! Ah well! My dear, you were right, when you told me that I'd thought about it myself. It is, indeed, the only way to rid myself of her.

"But, unfortunately - you see that I don't hesitate to use the word - unfortunately, it's impossible, because she's told me that she wrote her will and, predicting I might be tempted to accelerate the course of her existence, or rather to interrupt it brusquely, she inscribed, among her final bequests, that of having an autopsy, after her death, by doctors appointed by her whose names I don't know, but whom I have every reason to suspect are my personal enemies.

"Then she declared that should any trace of poison be discovered, her sole heir, whom she has not named to me, and who must also certainly not be one of my friends, would be charged with publishing certain documents which I was weak enough to allow her to steal, which would place me in a very tricky situation with regard to my people, and with certain other powers.

"As a result, my dear Rurick, you must wipe from your

slate, or rather from your mind, the idea of ridding me, by poison or by any other manner of violent death, of that accursed Barbara, who is destined to cling to me in perpetuity. Luckily she's not a jealous type, and she leaves me to act more or less freely, otherwise, life would be unbearable."

And changing the subject suddenly, he said in a light, almost chatty tone, "Are we going to the Moulin Rouge 'revue' this evening?"

"Absolutely, sire."

"That's good…"

His closest advisor said, "From the report that one of my secretaries whom I sent on reconnaissance gave me, it's a rather fine show."

"Pretty girls?"

"It's teeming with them, and I believe that Your Majesty will have an embarrassment of choice."

"Oh! My dear friend," replied Boris, in a rather weary tone, "I must admit that I'm beginning to tire of all those hectic, wriggling, over-painted dolls. The backstage odour, which those ladies bring with them to the private rooms, particularly sickens me.

"Anyway, you must have seen that for a while now, I've not thrown a handkerchief to any of those young ladies of any category, who strive to please us and to attract my attention, by all sorts of simpering with which I'm over-saturated."

"That's true, sire," declared Rupert, "I even wondered whether Your Majesty might be fatigued; but your robust health would rather seem to prove the opposite."

Boris I sneered. "Although I'm not descended from Henri IV, that famous king of France who was such a rough lifter of petticoats, I shan't hide the fact that I remain a

Green Gallant."

"My congratulations, sire."

"Only, here's the thing, I've been spoiled, and I'm becoming extremely particular. What I need, you see - oh! I'm not asking you to seek her out - is a tasty fruit, a young girl, a true young girl."

"A worker?" asked the old courtier.

"That wouldn't displease me," replied the king, "if I was sure she hadn't yet turned bad."

"We could see about that," said Rurick.

"After all, I'm not insisting," declared Boris I, "what if we came across one who had a father, or a brother, or even several, who might come to demand a reckoning? In France, there's not a great deal of respect for kings and they'd be only too happy to provoke a scandal which would put me in a difficult position."

"Your Majesty is prudence personified."

"No, you see, Rupert, what I need… is a young and charming woman, belonging to a bourgeois family, and timorous as a result, would, out of respect for their name, be careful not to spark a scene and content themselves with weeping silently for their dear child's 'stolen' virtue.

"I've no intention, anyway, of behaving like a swine with regards to the future lady. I'll be careful to arrange matters in such a way that neither she or her family will have any cause to complain."

Baron Rurick replied, "I don't see why Your Majesty couldn't give himself this satisfaction very soon. All the same, I'll allow myself to advise you not to make yourself known as Boris I, King of Sokovia, to your future conquest. Your Majesty is, in any case, a handsome enough man to be loved in his own right."

"There, my friend, you go off the rails entirely," declared the Count d'Esseck, "loved in my own right! I'm under no illusions on that subject. Even if that was the case, I wouldn't want it. I've always had an instinctive horror of anything which could resemble an idyll. I like to keep things tidy, clear, practical, and, ever eager for new and refined sensations, I have no intention of lingering in soppy and insignificant intrigues. You grasp my meaning, my dear Rupert?"

"Perfectly, sire."

"Do you have any fresh counsel for me?" asked the royal driver, with an ironic smile.

"My God! No, sire."

"You're right, and I'll admit quite frankly that it would not have been listened to."

Rurick didn't react; his soul was as supple as his spine.

The king asked, "Can I count on you?"

"As ever, sire."

"Then unleash your usual hunting pack, and I hope it will soon put me on the trail of the charming quarry that I look forward to enjoying."

2 FRANCINE

The car, after having hurtled down the coast of Saint-Cloud, crossed the bridge and headed down Avenue de Longchamp.

Night was beginning to fall; several cars were crossing this path; some had lit their lanterns. The king had to moderate his speed. But suddenly, blinded by the glare of a headlight that a driver, or rather a roadhog, had just lit, he responded by reflex, turning the wheel slightly to the right and, in the time it took to apply the brakes, he hit a cyclist, who, knocked from his bike, was sent violently to the pavement.

Boris stopped at once.

"I think there's been a prang," he said. "Rurick, go and see!"

The counsellor got out of the car and headed towards the injured party, who was already surrounded by several pedestrians.

He was a young worker of around seventeen or eighteen years, on his way home from work. He had fainted and bore a wound on his head which was bleeding profusely. Naturally, as always, the growing crowd was beginning to curse the clumsy driver, unaware they were addressing their epithets to one of the crowned heads of Europe.

Boris, impassive, remained silent, because he had no wish, especially in such circumstances, to give up his anonymity.

A policeman from Bois de Boulogne, who was passing by chance, approached and ordered the crowd to quiet down.

But his intervention was unsuccessful. Voices clamoured, "It's his fault… it's his fault…"

"He was going too fast…"

"The cyclist didn't have time to get out of his way…"

"These high-born people think they can do what they like… just because they have cars that cost three hundred thousand quid, they don't have to crush the poor…"

"He deserves to be chucked in the Seine, along with his motor…"

The policeman climbed on the running board and asked Boris, who was beginning to think that things were turning rather nasty for him, "First, your papers?"

"Here they are," said Boris I calmly, taking from his pocket a wallet, from which he took out a grey card and a driving permit and gave them to the policeman.

He examined them carefully.

"Count d'Esseck," he said, "are you a Parisian?"

"No," replied Boris, "I'm originally from Sokovia."

The guard continued. "Your papers are in order, it's the manner in which you've pranged this poor chap…"

"It's not my fault," replied King Boris.

"Oh! Oh! Oh! Oh! Oh!" screamed the mob.

Then, with a resonant voice, which drowned out the cries of protest, Boris spoke in an authoritative tone, which subdued the demonstrators at once.

"I tell you, it's not my fault. It was a driver who blinded me with his headlight, and caused me to give an unfortunate jerk to the wheel. But never fear, I'll make amends for my involuntary error. And though my moral responsibility must not be called into question, I'm quite prepared to compensate this unfortunate…"

But the shouting grew angrier.

"No… no… that's not true… liar… scoundrel… wastrel… crusher!"

Fists were raised at the king of Sokovia. The policeman, overwhelmed, was on the point of giving into public pressure, when suddenly a young couple rushed from the middle of the crowd, crying out, "We were there, we saw everything, and this gentleman is telling the truth!"

"Who are you?"

"Here's my card," replied the young man, passing it straight to the Count d'Esseck and adding, "I'm ready to testify, monsieur, as well as my fiancée here, that the accident happened just as you said and that the true guilty party is not you, but that roadhog who was quick to vanish!"

Nothing is more fickle than a crowd, especially in Paris. This intervention, as sincere as it was courageous, was enough for an immediate about-turn among the audience. No one, now, was thinking of injuring the Count d'Esseck. Those who had been the most ardent, and we'll add the most vulgar, became those who, quite the reverse, had been much more reserved in their judgement. And one of them cried out, as though he was speaking in the name of others, inflicting a well-deserved lesson on himself:

"It's always the same, those who saw nothing shout the loudest and repeat lies. Just because someone's bourgeois, it doesn't mean they're a murderer!"

Meanwhile, Boris had looked at the card that the young man had given him. It was inscribed thus:

Robert SANTENOIS
Electrical engineer
187, Avenue des Ternes
Paris

He tried to thank the lad for his selfless intervention, but for a moment he was speechless. Close to the engineer stood a young girl quite pink with emotion, but both beautiful and pretty as only a Frenchwoman can be, which goes double for Parisians. A delicious smile parted her lips.

Boris believed that it was directed at him, and he took great comfort from it. Then, leaning towards Robert Santenois, he said, "Is this mademoiselle your fiancée?"

"Yes, monsieur."

"Congratulations," said the king, with heavy emphasis.

And he added, "Here's my card. I would be delighted to receive an invitation to your wedding."

He held out his card, in the name of the Count d'Esseck, to Robert who, very much a man of the world, slipped it into his wallet without glancing at it. And, saluting the king, he was about to withdraw with his fiancée, when Rurick intervened, announcing, "The wound doesn't seem to be serious; however, it necessitates this boy's urgent transportation to a hospital. I've stopped several cars, but no one seems to want to take care of it."

Boris, who intended to be completely reconciled with public favour, said in a very loud voice, so as to be heard by everyone, "I must insist on taking this poor soul myself. It's my duty. But I'm a foreigner and I don't know Paris's hospitals very well; I don't know where to take him?"

The engineer declared, "From here, that would be Beaujon, monsieur."

"Beaujon… Beaujon…" repeated Boris, apparently

unaware not only of the name of the Farmer General who had given his name to the hospital[5], but even the location of this house of healing.

"I see, monsieur, that you're embarrassed," intervened the engineer, "I could show you the way."

"Monsieur, I wouldn't want to put you out," observed Boris.

"It's no problem at all," affirmed Robert. "Mademoiselle and I were going, indeed, to take the boat to get back to Paris."

"I would be sorry to deprive you of such a delightful walk."

"Not at all; in fact we'll be very happy to have the opportunity to be of service, not only to you, but also and above all to an injured man."

"I owe you an infinite debt," declared the king.

And turning to Rurick, he added, "Fetch the victim and have him carried into the car. Monsieur will sit beside me in order to guide me, and Mademoiselle will sit with you, inside the car, where you can take care of the invalid."

Some passers-by carried the cyclist. He was placed on the cushions. He had come to his senses and, at once, he was fearful, saying, "I think I have a broken arm and some bruising… I'll have to take a few weeks of forced leave."

---

[5] Nicolas Beaujon (1718-1786). A staggeringly wealthy private banker, who became a Farmer General. Prior to the Revolution, tax collection was "farmed out" to private individuals who collected taxes to a set quota, and pocketed any surplus legally. Beaujon Hospital, founded in 1784, was intended for poor orphans. This late act of philanthropy wasn't enough to deter a mob from desecrating his tomb during the French Revolution, and scattering his ashes. The hospital is still open, but it relocated to Clichy in 1935, six years after this book was published, so don't go taking Chantecoq selfies at the wrong building.

And he added, "All the same, I didn't expect to be transported to a hospital this evening, in a luxury car."

Then suddenly he cried, "What about my bike, good God? Some weirdos must already have pinched it."

He moved as though to get out of the car, but Baron de Rurick stopped him, saying, "It was in a pretty sorry state. Calm down, you'll be compensated, you can buy yourself a much nicer one."

"You know what I want…" cried the wounded man.

"Speak…"

"Very well! I'd be broadly content if I could buy myself a motorbike."

Baron Rupert replied, "I think I can assure you that your wish will be promptly realised."

"I see that I've fallen on high society, and on society which has a good heart. Which is rare. In any case, monsieur, I don't know your name, but you can be sure of one thing, that, if you give me the means to buy myself a motorbike, I won't go and test it in Bois de Boulogne, so as not to pull off the same trick and, next time, you'd buy me a superb six cylinder Talbot, the latest model, with the special chassis and double windscreen-wipers…"

Then, looking at the young girl sitting next to him, he said, "Are you the gentleman's wife, by any chance?"

"No," replied the young girl, "I simply witnessed the accident."

"Oh! You're a *witness*? I hope you're not going to be against me?"

"No one," replied Robert Santenois's fiancée, "*no one* will be speaking against you."

"All in good time… So, it only remains for me to reveal my name, qualities and profession so we can all be friends:

I'm Isidore Martineau, aka Dry Tripe. I'm an electrician, and I live with my family up in Saint-Cloud. I won't ask you to visit because, really, in terms of luxury, our house leaves something to be desired. But I thank you all the same, after having broken my bike, for not vanishing over the horizon as so many others would have done."

Amused by this pure-blooded Parisian's language, maintaining truly remarkable courage and even gaiety, despite the harsh challenge he had undergone and the pain he must still be suffering, his neighbour replied.

"Since you've introduced yourself to us, I'll also tell you my name. I'm Mademoiselle Francine Gardannes. I have no nickname, and while you live in the heights of Saint-Cloud, I reside on Montmartre! My profession: artist and painter."

"In that case, mademoiselle, perhaps you could paint my portrait?"

"Sadly, I only paint flowers."

"As a flower, I'd make a rather pitiful painting; but forgive my indiscretion."

Then, in a low voice, he whispered to Francine, who was finding the injured man more and more pleasant, "Who's the old codger sitting opposite you?"

"I don't know," replied Francine.

Monsieur de Rurick, with the sharp hearing of an experienced diplomat, undoubtedly caught the words that young Isidore uttered, or understood his meaning from his facial expression or lip movements. He replied with a smile that was friendly, but a little strained, "My turn to introduce myself; I'm secretary to the Count d'Esseck, who's presently behind the wheel."

"Yes," said Dry Tripe, "the weirdo - Oh! Forgive me, that slipped out - the gentleman who failed to knock my teeth out? Well, it's funny, I'm not judging him, since you offered, in his name, to buy me a motorbike with, naturally, expenses for the injury. In fact I like him a lot, your Count de… I forget what you said…"

"Esseck. Very well…"

"That's not a French name, is it?"

"No, it's the name of a great Sokovian family."

"Sokovia, Sokovia," Isidore repeated. "I've heard talk of that backwater, but I've really no idea where it is. I've never been that great at geography: France is the capital of Panama; fine, after that, best not ask me too much.

"And then, since the War, Europe's been cut into so many slices that I no longer understand anything, the Slovaks, the Czechs, the Yugos, the Slavs… I'm lost!

"But never mind, seeing as I'll have my motorbike!"

Noticing the young man sitting next to the Count d'Esseck, he said, "Him now, he's surely a Frenchman. Do you know him, mademoiselle?"

"Yes," replied Francine, smiling, "that's my fiancé. I'll give you his details: he's Robert Santenois. He's an engineer for Paris's Central Electricity Company."

Isidore interrupted. "Electrician… ah! That's perfect, I was just looking for a job, seeing as I only earn beans at mine, which aren't even good to cook. I'd be terribly happy to join his business.

"It seems a decent firm, and I'm not a skiver, especially when I have both arms! When I need to, I put in a decent day's work and I only work the English week when there's no work![6]

"I'm not a grumbler, I've a good character! So long as I get my motorbike… and, from time to time, go to the

---

[6] It's sad to reflect that it used to be the French who mocked the amount of time off enjoyed by British workers.

39

cinema… Ah! Cinema, I won't deny that's my pleasure… and you, mademoiselle?"

"I like the cinema too."

"And you, monsieur?"

"Me too."

Delighted at finding listeners whose tastes seemed to conform to his own so closely, Dry Tripe continued.

"Only, I'm going to say it: I don't like American films. Whether it's cowboys, workers, peasants, men of the world, ministers and even Presidents, they can't spend two whole minutes without punching each other in the kisser… sorry, mademoiselle, if I had been talking about you, I'd have said: in the face!

"In the end, all those people fighting for a yes, or a no… it gets boring, while French films… ah! They're amazing. First, there's interesting stories, and then, our actors are much better than theirs. They chew less tobacco, you see! And at least we have some beautiful countryside to show, beautiful chateaux, beautiful country houses, not always wooden houses!

"There's only one American that I really rate: that's Charlot. He's worthy of being one of ours, because he's from everywhere, and he has good eyes, a good smile… he must be a decent guy, or else I don't know my own self."[7]

While the man with a broken arm, who appeared to be blessed with an inexhaustible verve, continued to recount his opinions to Francine Gardannes and Count Rupert, the car had stopped in front of Beaujon Hospital. Robert Santenois was getting out, saying, "Wait a moment, I'll take care of the necessary formalities."

---

[7] Charlie Chaplin (1899-1977), who was at the height of his fame at this point with films such as *The Gold Rush* (1925), and *City Lights* (1928). AKA "Charlot" in France, although he was British.

"Of course," agreed the Count d'Esseck.

And turning to the car's back seat, he said to Isidore, "My friend! You're not in too much pain?"

"Not too much, Count. All the same, I can't tell you that I'm well; but all in all, it's tolerable. Apart from the fact I've got a broken arm, a bit of a black eye, and a few cuts on my face, it's no big deal. What's more, your secretary says you're going to offer me compensation, which would stop any frills or dramas."

"No, my lad."

"Oh! However, as long as I have my motorbike…"

"Your motorbike? Boris echoed him.

"Yes, your secretary promised me."

"Ah! Sorry," replied Baron Rupert, who was trying to limit his responsibility with regard to his master, whose generosity he knew to be rather capricious.

But Boris, delighted to be getting away with the matter so cheaply, continued, "Oh yes, yes, understood; you'll get your motorbike, my friend."

And drawing two thousand franc notes from his wallet, he gave them to his victim, saying, "Take that, my lad."

Francine passed the notes and gave them to Dry Tripe, who looked at them with satisfaction.

But, suddenly seized by a slight worry, he said, "Forgive me, Count. Only, a motorbike, they cost more than two grand… To get a tool that really zaps along, you need five thousand, or more…"

Boris smiled. "Ah, these Parisians," he said, "they're wonderfully amusing!"

Then he continued. "Don't worry, my lad. These two thousand francs are just an advance on the indemnity that I'm proposing to offer you. As to the motorbike, ah well, that will be a present that I'll be delighted to give you, since you've shown yourself to be so reasonable and you've not tried for a moment to be even slightly disagreeable."

Isidore, delighted, radiant, beaming like an angel, cried out, "Ah, that's pretty sweet, Count! And surely if all rich people were like you, there would be less misery, fewer malcontents, fewer revolts, and everyone would ask only to go about their business peacefully; because I consider that, so long as one has one's motorbike, one mustn't ask for anything more."

"You'll have it, my boy. I promise you personally it'll be the most beautiful motorbike I can find."

While speaking, Boris, instead of looking at his victim, had turned his gaze towards Francine who, for her part, was smiling down at the brave Martineau.

Baron Rupert, who knew his master better than anyone, said to himself, "Why's he being so generous towards this simple worker, there must be a serious reason for it? I believe I guess the reason; he wants to please this young woman opposite me, and I wouldn't be surprised, given his current state of mind, if she hadn't already made a considerable impression on him.

"I hope I'm mistaken, because, if I'm right, I suspect that I'll soon be launched into an adventure in the course of which I'll risk all sorts of bother."

Robert Santenois was coming out of the hospital, and said to Boris, "Everything is arranged."

And addressing the injured man, he added, "Do you feel strong enough to get out of the car?"

"And how!" replied Dry Tripe.

"If not, don't put yourself out," replied the engineer, "because nothing would be easier than to call over two stretcher carriers."

"Oh, no! No problem… thank you, I'm not a wet chicken."

Indeed, without needing anyone's help, Martineau got out of the car, his arm bent and his hand in his shirt's armpit, and, turning towards to the prince, he said to him, "I daren't ask you to visit me, but, truly, it would do me good to hear from you."

And returning to Santenois, he said, "Goodbye, mademoiselle! Goodbye, monsieur secretary! And onwards! They can put me on the billiard table, I don't care! What harm can it do me, since I'm going to have my motorbike!"

And he vanished into the doorway with Santenois, who was intending to take him to the front desk.

Francine, who had also got out of the car, was going to follow him, but Boris called her back with an extremely deferential and courteous tone. "Mademoiselle, where are you going?"

"To join my fiancé," Francine replied.

"Oh! I beg you, wait," asked the Count d'Esseck. "The least I can do is to drive you both home."

"Oh! Monsieur, I wouldn't want to abuse…"

"It's the least I can do, after the help you and Monsieur Santenois have given me!"

Boris fell silent; then, observing that the young girl was accepting the invitation that he had just extended, he continued.

"You're going to think, mademoiselle, that I'm very indiscreet; but it seems to me that your face is not entirely unknown to me and that I've already had the honour of meeting you, whether at the theatre, or at the races…"

"Not the races," replied Francine, "because I never go there; but perhaps at the theatre."

"Quite recently, at a performance at the Comédie on Champs-Elysées, weren't you sitting on the front row of the orchestra seats, next to a lady with white hair, who seemed very distinguished?"

"Indeed, monsieur," acknowledged Robert's fiancée, not without a certain astonishment, "I was at that performance with my mother."

"You see, I wasn't mistaken."

"You have an extremely remarkable memory for faces, monsieur."

"Permit me, mademoiselle, to tell you there's no need for a great memory to preserve the memory of a young lady as charming as you."

Baron Rupert, who hadn't missed a single word of this dialogue, was thinking, "This time, he's trapped. What an idea he had, that imbecile cyclist, throwing himself under our wheels like that. I'd honestly have given him a Rolls-Royce to avoid that; because I know my Boris, if he wants this girl, he'll have her! By what means? I hardly dare imagine... it's going to be frightening!

"Why can't this amorous ogre content himself with those tarts, who claim to be women of the world, and with those women of the world who act like tarts? He's already found out what it cost him getting ensnared by an adventuress such as the Duchess de Castrovillari. But with adventurers of that sort, you can always get your way with some money, while with this little one, it's much more serious: she certainly loves her fiancé, and her fiancé loves her too. That can lead to formidable complications.

"Truly, Boris has better things to do than try to break these two hearts, to wither this idyll. I'm not worth much, I know, but all the same, there are some acts so shameful that one ought to refuse to carry them out, however low one has fallen into disgrace, vice, and oblivion.

"But to try and make this crowned brute see reason… to disobey him, then! Not only do I risk losing my situation in this game, but I'm also risking my liberty! I already know so much about him that Boris might not mind ridding himself of me, and I intend to live."

While the King of Sokovia's counsellor was quietly engaged in these rather sombre prognostications, Robert Santenois had left the hospital and returned to the car.

He was preparing to take leave of the two foreigners, when Francine said to him, "Monsieur has been so kind as to offer us a lift home. He insisted with such good grace that I didn't think I ought to refuse; and as you're dining at my house tonight, it will only be one trip for him."

Addressing Boris, who hadn't taken his eyes from the young girl for a moment, Robert said, "Monsieur, I'm truly dazzled by your generosity."

"You accept, then?"

"I couldn't do otherwise," retorted the engineer, "since Mademoiselle Francine Gardannes has decided."

He climbed back on the seat next to Boris, who started his engine, saying, "Monsieur, would you please give me the address?"

"It's 37, Rue Saint-Vincent. Access to the street is not very easy."

Boris replied, "I know Montmartre very well… calm yourself, I won't commit any errors."

Indeed, without the slightest hesitation, even taking a relatively quiet route, such as are few and far between in our beautiful city of Paris, the Count d'Esseck arrived quite quickly at the indicated address, where Robert got out first.

The Count d'Esseck followed him and offered his hand to Francine, who had opened the door.

After helping her to climb out, he raised his hat, and bowed respectfully to the young girl, saying, "Mademoiselle, my compliments."

Then he held out his hand to the engineer. "My compliments, monsieur," he said, "your fiancée is exquisite, to my eyes she represents the true Parisian woman, simple, charming... you're a lucky man and I'm sure that you'll be a happy husband."

Somewhat impressed by the cordial tone and lordly air that the fake Count d'Esseck had adopted, Robert replied, "Thank you, monsieur, all best wishes..."

Gracious and smiling, Francine said to Rurick, who also bowed before her, "Above all, gentlemen, don't forget the motorbike!"

"I'm forgetting nothing, mademoiselle," replied the count.

Robert and Francine entered a pretty house, flanked by a small garden.

The king got back behind the wheel and Baron Rupert took his place next to him.

They returned to the king's house, which was situated, as described above, in Neuilly, Boulevard Maillot.

The king didn't unclench his teeth until they reached l'Etoile.

This silence worried his counsellor all the more as he was interpreting it as evidence of the amorous preoccupations which were already assailing his master.

He wasn't mistaken; because, while going down Avenue de la Grande Armée, Boris, who had slowed down before testing the water, murmured in a voice which seemed deliberately muted, "Rurick, you saw that girl, didn't you?"

"Yes, sire."

Boris, in a tone full of an authority that was so much more formidable for being cold and calculated, said, "My dear Rupert, this child must be mine! You have eight days to arrange it."

3 THE AMBUSH

Let's now enter the intimate abode of Madame Gardannes and her daughter.

We already know that they lived in a charming new house on Rue Saint-Vincent, that's to say right at the top of Montmartre.

Madame Gardannes was the widow of an architect who, through his talent and work, had succeeded in acquiring a modest fortune, which could have been more considerable, if he'd proved to be more avid.

But Francine's father was one of those modest men who want to owe nothing to anything but their own merit.

They had acquired a pleasant lifestyle, before they were hounded by a less scrupulous competitor; but they never attained the great summits of glory and money which are demanded by those who are trying to manage a ceaseless tension between their ambitious mind, and sometimes even some processes which are repugnant to all honest consciences.

Nevertheless, when Monsieur Gardannes, following a long and serious illness, departed his loved ones, he was able to leave them with the satisfaction of having done his duty, and the certainty that he left behind a widow and a daughter who were sheltered from all hardship.

Francine wasn't one of those young girls who dream of a completely mundane lifestyle.

From a very young age she felt drawn irresistibly towards the arts, and particularly towards painting. Horrified at the gossips in salons, with those afternoon teas where one passes one's time adulating the persons present, and tearing to pieces those who are absent, and having little inclination towards sports such as tennis, which might merit both her approval and her respect when practised in moderation, but which become an odious encumbrance when snobbery gets involved, she preferred an intellectual and purely artistic lifestyle.

Encouraged by her mother, a woman of good heart and perfect common sense, she had therefore been able to follow the vocation for which she was destined.

She had taken lessons from the best masters who, interested by her genuine aptitudes and special gifts, had advised her to specialise in the painting of flowers, where she excelled.

Her canvasses in no way resembled those gaudy images worthy at best of featuring on the cover of bad almanacs.

No, she painted living flowers, sweet-smelling flowers, whose sparkle and colour, interpreted by her, not only drew the eye, but earned fervent admiration from all true connoisseurs.

Her first submission to the Salon[8] had been much commented upon. Several art dealers came to find her, to ask her to work for them under highly attractive conditions; but Francine, who had that great strength of not needing to earn

[8] The official art exhibition of the Société des Artistes Français.

a living, declined those propositions.

She wanted to remain independent, and faithful to the principle that art is not produced on demand, and that a true artist must work only when they feel truly inspired.

That evening, Madame Gardannes and Francine were sitting in the pretty studio, furnished simply but with great taste, where the young artist spent most of her time.

Madame Gardannes was lying on a chaise longue, because she was suffering from an attack of rheumatism in her knees which, without being of serious concern, had already immobilised her for several months.

She could hardly drag herself from her bedroom to her daughter's studio, yet the two were separated only by a narrow corridor.

Madame Gardannes was asking Francine, who was reading an evening newspaper, "Would you be so kind, darling, as to play me a little music?"

Francine, who adored her mother, went over to the piano which she opened, saying, "What would you like me to play?"

"The *Moonlight Sonata*..."

Francine, who was almost as skilled a musician as she was a painter, immediately began to perform Beethoven's admirable piece, which her mother had requested.

She interpreted it, that sublime fragment, which seems to express all human suffering, all the regrets of a soul who flies away, at the same time as the despair of beloved beings, who survive it, not only with superb style, but with an interior emotion that only true artists possess.

Madame Gardannes, her eyes half-closed, listened to her daughter with a joy that was doubled by maternal pride.

When Francine finished, she left the piano and returned to her mother, who she kissed tenderly.

Madame Gardannes replied, "You've never expressed better that admirable piece that I always listen to with such contemplation. It's hard, if not impossible, to interpret Beethoven any better."

"Mother," cried the young girl, "you really are far too indulgent towards me.

"Oh no, I assure you."

While speaking, Francine's eyes wandered towards a Louis XVI clock that hung on the wall.

Her mother said, smiling at her kindly, "You're checking the time and you've realised, no doubt, that the hands aren't turning as fast as you'd like. You're waiting for Robert."

"I'll admit that I'm beginning to feel a little anxious. He ought to be here already."

Madame Gardannes objected, "Perhaps he couldn't take the train he intended. The business that took him to Rouen today was of the greatest importance, it's likely he didn't have time to finish it."

Francine replied, "If that was the case, I know Robert; he'd have found a way to telephone me, or for someone to notify me, because he knows how anxious I am when I'm waiting for him."

Half an hour passed. It was midnight. Sadly, almost painfully, the young girl said, "Now I'm sure of it, he won't be coming now."

And she added, sighing, "Just as long as he's not had an accident!"

Madame Gardannes was trying to reassure her, when a bell rang in the hallway next door.

"Perhaps that's him," cried Francine.

"Let's just say that it is him," said her mother.

Francine was already in the hallway and opening the door, preparing to welcome her fiancé with all the impulsiveness of her deep tenderness.

It wasn't Robert Santenois who faced her, but a stranger, a man of around fifty years old, clean-shaven, with greying brown hair, very properly dressed, and with a proper and even reserved appearance.

"Mademoiselle Gardannes?" he asked, raising his hat.

"That's me, monsieur," responded the young artist, who had paled, because she had a premonition of catastrophe.

"Mademoiselle," he said, "I have a few things to tell you. I'm Monsieur Romero Levitz, and I'm the director of the Franco-Czech clinic on Boulevard Delessert."

"Come in, monsieur," Francine invited him, more and more overwhelmed.

Now she was sure of it, Robert must have been involved in a serious accident!

She showed the visitor into the studio where she introduced him to her mother.

He, after bowing respectfully to Madame Gardannes, continued in French that was correct, but not without traces of a foreign accent.

"I beg your pardon, ladies, for disturbing you at such a late hour. But I was sent by Monsieur Robert Santenois."

He stopped for a moment, casting a piercing gaze at the two women, whose faces betrayed their concern; then he continued in a voice full of compassionate inflections.

"I beg you, ladies, not to be overly alarmed. Monsieur Santenois isn't in any danger of dying, far from it. On returning from Rouen, he was struck down, between Vernon and Mantes, with an attack of acute appendicitis, he had to be transported immediately to our clinic, where one of his friends, Professor Denoir, the famous surgeon, will be operating on him shortly.

"Monsieur Santenois, who didn't have the strength to

write, asked me to come to you, to warn you what had become of him, and to reassure you not to worry unduly.

"He expressed one desire to me, however: that, mademoiselle, is to know you are not far from him during the operation."

"Director," replied the young artist, "I was just preparing to return to the clinic with you. Will you let me, mother?"

"My darling," said Madame Gardannes, "I wouldn't want to delay you for a single moment, or deprive your fiancé of this touching consolation."

"So much more so," replied the director, "as there's no danger, and, from what our invalid has said, I'm certain that he'll be very happy, when he awakes, to see his fiancée at his bedside. Consequently, if Mademoiselle Gardannes would like to join me in my car, I'm at her disposal."

"Doctor, I accept," said Francine. "Give me a moment to put on a hat, and a coat!"

She went to kiss her mother and said, "I'll wake the chambermaid, so she can help you to bed."

"Thank you, my darling."

Francine disappeared like a shadow.

Certainly, she was still quite overwhelmed by what she had just learned; but, contrary to her initial fears, nothing was lost yet. And it was with less fear that she envisaged the situation, which was certainly painful, but was not one of those which sows irredeemable despair in you.

Quickly, she went back to the studio, held her mother tenderly in her arms for a moment, and then left with Monsieur Romero Levitz who, in the few moments he was alone with Madame Gardannes, had only confirmed to her the exactitude of his affirmations.

Francine and the director got in a car parked by the pavement, which was driven by a chauffeur in a dark uniform, and with a polite attitude.

On the way, Francine asked her visitor numerous questions about her fiancé.

Monsieur Levitz replied with complete complacency, then, suddenly, she glanced through the window and said, "It seems to me that your driver isn't taking the road to Boulevard Delessert."

"Indeed," replied the director, "it's been arranged that I'd pass by Professor Deloir's house to fetch him too. It saves time."

Francine made no objection to this response, which seemed entirely satisfying, and soon the car stopped before a house, situated on Chaussée de la Muette and which, surrounded by a garden, was isolated from the neighbouring houses.

"Mademoiselle," said Romero, "would you be so good as to accompany me, because I can tell you now: Professor Deloir doesn't want to be disturbed. He's talking about sending one of his colleagues and I would be particularly grateful to you, if you would persuade him to operate himself, because, in such cases, it's better to deal with the master than with his students."

"I couldn't ask for more, monsieur. I'm quite ready," replied Francine, "to do anything required for my fiancé to receive all necessary treatment as soon as possible."

"I'm sure," retorted Monsieur Levitz, "that your intervention will do the trick, and I'm convinced that we'll soon be taking the great surgeon in this car."

The director climbed out, offered his hand to Francine, and rang at the house's front gate.

It was opened rather quickly.

A porter came out into the night, asking, "Who are you, and what do you want?"

Romero replied, "I'm Monsieur Levitz, director of the clinic on Boulevard Delessert, and Mademoiselle is the fiancée of one of our patients. Monsieur the professor is expecting us, anyway. Here's my card! Take it to him at once!"

Romero held out a business card to the porter who, after having shut the gate, led the nocturnal visitors to the modern building's entrance, which he guarded.

Behind the windows, some lights announced that the house was not yet asleep.

The porter pressed a buzzer next to the front door, which opened at once. A liveried footman appeared. The porter gave him the director's card, saying, "Take that to your master."

The footman obeyed at once, after indicating to Monsieur Levitz and the young artist a red velvet bench on which they sat.

The porter stayed there, as though to watch these people whom he didn't know. Three minutes later, the footman returned, announcing, "If Mademoiselle and Monsieur would follow me, they will be received immediately."

Following the footman, they climbed a marble staircase, whose cast iron banister curled in capricious modern arabesques. They arrived on a landing, decorated with several statues, placed on plinths, which all represented nude women.

Francine was too worried about Robert to pay this strange decor the slightest attention.

The footman lifted a magnificent Aubusson tapestry, turned a door handle, and said, simply, "This way, monsieur, and mademoiselle."

Francine took a few steps. She found herself in a vast lounge, with ultra-modern decoration and extremely dim lights, in which she could make out, among the bizarrely-shaped furniture, to which it was difficult to give any qualification, a tall man who approached her at once.

Dumbfounded by this strange scene, Francine turned back towards he who had brought her to this place; but she didn't see him, for the simple reason that he hadn't entered the room.

More and more intimidated, she stayed rooted to the spot, asking the man who was continuing to move towards her slowly, very slowly, and whose face, through the surrounding shadows, she was having trouble making out, "Do I have the honour of meeting Professor Deloir…"

She didn't finish. The person, now very close to her, pressed a switch, placed next to his hand.

At once the room was flooded with bright light, and Francine gave a cry of shock. She recognised the Count d'Esseck.

"What, monsieur, is that you?" she said. "What's the meaning of this?"

"My dear child," replied the king of Sokovia, "I'm going to tell you. Please take the trouble of sitting down, and I'll explain why, instead of finding yourself with the famous Professor Deloir, you're meeting me this evening."

Sensing a trap, the young girl fell silent, and remained immobile.

Boris, with feline gestures, tried to take her hand, but she moved away.

"What?" said the unworthy king indignantly, "you're afraid? Do you imagine, my dear child, that you have something to fear from me? I swear to you, I intend, rather, to be agreeable to you."

"In that case," replied Francine baldly, beginning to get a grip on herself, "why have you brought me here by means of a process which has every appearance to me of an ambush?"

Boris cried out, "You use very bold words for a young girl of your age: an ambush, let's rather say a ruse, and a ruse which is so much more forgivable as it was inspired, I can't keep it from you any longer, by the deep and sincere love that you've aroused in me."

"Me?" exclaimed the young artist, whose face was flushing purple.

"Yes, you."

"Monsieur, you've seen me only once."

"That was enough to receive what they commonly call the thunderbolt."

"No, monsieur," Francine replied with dignity, "you don't love me. If you truly loved me, you wouldn't have employed a trick whose cowardice reveals clearly the kind of man you are."

"Oh! Oh! Let's not get angry, I beg you. Anyway, I've decided to arm myself with patience and I'll bear all your accusations and injuries, because I'm certain you will come to regret them all too quickly and that you won't be long in coming to realise that I alone can assure your happiness."

"No, monsieur," retorted the young artist, more and more sure of herself, "it's futile to insist. I've given my heart, my soul, my whole life to a man who surpasses you with the nobility of his soul and the generosity of his sentiments."

"Yes," replied Boris, in a tone tinged with irony, "that handsome young man, who was with you the other day, when we took that imbecile to Beaujon Hospital. He's a fine-looking chap, and I have no pretensions of rivaling him. But what is he, after all, a poor engineer who barely earns twenty-five thousand francs a year, no future, and who won't take long to become a grumpy husband, jealous of your success as a woman and as an artist, in a word, to poison your life."

Revolted, Francine retorted, "I forbid you to talk like that about the man I love."

Sneering nastily, Boris replied, "You love him! I see that, by Jove! You don't need to tell me. But does he love you?"

"I'm sure of that!"

"Poor blind thing! All those amorous protestations he makes, there's not a word of truth in them."

"Monsieur, I don't believe you!"

"I've made a very serious investigation. I acquired proof that Robert Santenois was attracted to you only by self-interest. Remember you're more than an honourable party. You have an attractive personal fortune. You have talent, a great deal of talent. You're already selling your paintings, if not at a huge price, then at more than acceptable rates and I'm convinced that, in two or three years, if you wanted to modernise your style, art dealers will be fighting for your art. All that represents both serious capital and very comfortable annuities.

"Come on, let's see, let me open your eyes, ready to cause you some pain, great pain; but the best operations are always the most radical. Your Robert Santenois cares so little for you that he is, at this moment, with a mistress in Rouen."

"That's not true…"

"I anticipated that response," replied Boris. "So I made sure to have on my person the flagrant proof that what I'm telling you is the complete truth."

He took from his wallet a folded letter which he gave to Francine, saying, "Read it, mademoiselle. Then tell me whether I've lied to you."

With a trembling hand, Francine took the missive that the Count d'Esseck was holding out to her, who then said, "First, look at the handwriting and tell me that's not your fiancé's hand."

"It certainly resembles it," acknowledged the young artist.

"Well, then! Read on," the sovereign invited her.

Francine read the following:

My darling Fifi,

It's agreed; on Friday, we'll both leave for Rouen.

I've given the pretext that I was called to that town on important business. The business in question being that we'll both spend some time together in peace.

I intend not to return to Paris until Monday during the day.

I'll tell you-know-who that I missed my last train.

Above all, don't be jealous anymore. This marriage is imposed on me by circumstances. I've many debts; my creditors are beginning to show their teeth and, if I don't satisfy them as promptly as possible and if they complain to my employer, I'll certainly lose my job.

I can only repeat, as I've already said so often, "Whatever happens, I'll always be your lover."

It would be impossible for me to get over you. I would prefer to be finished with life itself.

I send you a million kisses.

Until Friday morning, then. I'll telephone you with the train time, meet me at Gare Saint-Lazare.

Your Robert who loves you hopelessly.

Very calm, very self-controlled, Francine returned to Boris the letter, which was supposed to prove the betrayal of he in whom she had put all her faith.

"Well, then!" said Boris, a little surprised at her attitude, "what do you say to that? It doesn't seem to have made much of an impression."

With great composure, the young artist replied, "I'd like to know, before anything else, how this letter came into your hands. Was it this Mademoiselle Fifi who gave it to you... or sold it?"

"Allow me to say nothing of that. This document came into my possession in a fashion which concerns me alone and I have no right to compromise those who procured it for me."

"Well, monsieur," declared Francine, "the people who gave you or sold you this paper are having a laugh with you, or have robbed you."

"What are you saying?" the king of Sokovia said with a start.

"I'm saying," intoned the young artist firmly, "that this letter is a forgery."

"Prove it..."

"Ah! If I had a few lines of my fiancé's handwriting, I would convince you immediately, because there are flagrant discrepancies between the two hands. Truly whoever furnished you with this letter didn't give you good value for money."

"Mademoiselle," replied Boris, who was beginning to succumb to impatience and anger, "you are, I see, very difficult to persuade!"

"I'm a woman who sees clearly in her own heart, as well as in that of the man that she loves, and that permits me to unmask you entirely and to say to you: monsieur, enough, let's leave things there and never find yourself in my path again, Count d'Esseck or not; because I'd proclaim your infamy to your face and, however high on the social ladder, however powerful your connections, however numerous your friends, when they learn of your conduct towards me,

60

there's not one honest man - and there are still many honest people in France - who would judge your conduct other than as it deserves."

Turning on her heel, she made for the door. Boris grabbed her arm and, incapable of controlling himself any longer, exasperated by the desire which burned within him, he cried, "Mad, mad as you are, you don't see that you're setting aside your happiness."

"Setting aside happiness?" Francine repeated, "Would it be you, by any chance, who would provide me with that happiness?"

"Yes, me."

"You… you," thundered the young artist. "Even if I didn't love Robert Santenois, even if the letter that you showed me had been authentic, I'd rather live my whole life in misery, rather than receive even alms from such a vile creature as you."

Furious, Boris increased the pressure of his fingers around the young girl's arm.

"Let me go," she cried, "you're hurting me."

Then, bursting from a long-contained intoxication, the king hissed, "And you, do you imagine that you're not making me suffer in the most atrocious fashion. It's barely fifteen days since I met you and I've not seen you since! Not for one moment has your image ceased to haunt me, to obsess me; it was you I saw everywhere, before me, a living apparition which yet eluded me whenever I tried to grasp it. Well! Tonight I hold you, and I won't let you go."

Carried away by madness, he pulled Francine towards him and threw her on to the divan.

With a brutal hand, he tried to tear her bodice; but the girl had time to grab a little Japanese bronze, with which she gave the wretch's forehead a violent thump.

He fell to the ground and lay stunned on the carpet for a moment.

The young artist jumped up and hurried to the door. It was locked and the keyhole was empty.

Then she rushed to one of the lounge windows and opened it wide to scream for help. Meanwhile Boris had got up, and launched himself once again at Francine, who cried, "If you come near me and if you so much as touch me, I'll throw myself out of the window."

Whether he didn't believe this threat, or whether he'd lost all sense of reality, Boris continued to advance. Francine launched herself into the night. She would rather die than be dishonoured.

The amorous ogre stood for a moment, dazed, then he went to the window, leaned out, and saw, in the middle of a courtyard, his victim's body, which was lying unmoving.

Some drops of sweat appeared on his forehead. And, shaking himself, he said, "Damn! I believe I've gone a bit too far. This little drama isn't going to be easy to sort out."

4 BARBARA

He went over to press a buzzer. A few seconds later, a small door opened in one of the corners of the lounge, making way for the clinic's fake director who approached his sovereign with a respectful air.

The so-called Romero Levitz was none other than a certain Arad, chief of secret police whom the King of Sokovia kept close during his travels.

The king said simply, "The little one just flung herself from the window."

Arad didn't appear to display any emotion at this.

Doubtless he'd seen plenty of others.

He approached the window, which remained open. He leaned out, looked and, in an implacably cold tone, he said, "We must hope she's dead. It would make things much easier to sort out. I suggest Your Majesty return to your room. We'll go, Mako and I, to do the necessary. Your Majesty can be sure, even if that young person is still alive, everything will be taken care of.

"No one saw anything, or heard anything, as such, there is no scandal to be feared."

Chewing his lip, Boris returned to his rooms, without adding another word.

The chief of police had already disappeared and rejoined his colleague Mako, who was waiting in a neighbouring room.

At once, he began. "The king just made a huge cock-up."

"What's that, then?"

"You know that girl that he charged us with bringing to him? Well! Boris I acted in such a brutal fashion, as is his habit, that the kid threw herself out of the window and she's lying, right now, in a flowerbed. Quick, find a blanket large enough to wrap her up and join me in the garden, so we can take all the precautions made necessary by our dangerous boss's latest prank."

Mako left at once.

As to Arad, he went to the garden via the service stairs, which must have been secret, as he alone had the key, and he opened the door which led straight to the miniature park that surrounded the house.

He went to the flowerbed and knelt near Francine's body, which showed no further signs of life.

He leaned over her chest and listened.

At that moment, Mako, a short, dark and nervous man, returned with the blanket. Turning to him, Arad said, "She's alive."

"Damn!" grumbled the other policeman, "that's going to complicate things."

"No, no," corrected the chief of police, "you'll see, instead, everything's going to turn out fine. The main thing is not to lose our heads, and to get on with things as always."

While speaking, he had taken the blanket and covered the young girl's body with it. She, still unconscious, had not made any protest.

The surroundings were deserted. No one could have seen Francine fall from the window or Arad and Mako picking her up.

The topography and layout of the area lent itself admirably to envelop this drama, which had unfolded so briefly and tragically, in impenetrable mystery.

By the small service staircase, they carried Francine back to the lounge where the scene that we just described took place.

Arad lifted the blanket.

Francine gave a little cry.

"Just as I thought," said the policeman, "she's only injured."

Arad added, "What do we do with her? I can't decide anything without orders from the king."

Mako replied, "Find him. I'll watch over the girl, in case she wakes up and calls for help."

He went to the window which he closed, and Arad vanished through the door in the corner.

He hurried along a corridor and gave three discreet knocks on a door.

"Who's there?" called Boris's voice.

"Arad," the policeman responded.

The door opened at once and Boris appeared in the opening, pale, his features drawn, his lip flecked with foam.

He immediately waved his agent into his room, closing the door himself and, turning to him, he asked with an anxious air, "Dead?"

"No," replied Arad. "Alive, and I don't even think she's seriously injured. The flowerbed's soil bore the impact of her fall, and she'll regain consciousness very soon now."

Boris was silent. He seemed very perplexed.

He began to pace up and down in his room, his brain

boiling, looking for ideas.

Stopping suddenly in front of his confidant and his accomplice in his sad and lewd adventures, he said to him in a strident voice, "Arad, what would you do in my position?"

The policeman replied, "Sire, I'm only a humble servant. I couldn't offer you any advice…"

"Even if I ordered you to…"

"Sire, that's different."

"So speak, I want to hear you."

Arad continued in a more assured tone. "Sire, I'll begin by telling you that I would be just as embarrassed as you, because I see only two solutions to this unfortunate business: the first would consist of sending Mademoiselle Gardannes back to her mother, and then it's a scandal with all its consequences, unless the French government agrees to stifle this whole thing."

"They will agree," affirmed Boris, "I can assure you of that."

"Yes, but are they powerful enough to obtain the fiancée's silence, and her mother's? I doubt it."

Boris cried in the tone of an autocrat, who has a habit of seeing everything bow before him, "We'll give them a golden gag and they'll have to keep quiet."

"Your Majesty must permit me to doubt that," retorted the policeman. "During the investigation I made into this young girl, I observed that Madame Gardannes and Monsieur Santenois were formidable adversaries who would be very difficult and perhaps impossible to silence.

"When they learn you lured that young girl to this house, that you tried to coerce her with violence, and that she could escape you only by throwing herself from a window, I'm sure it's not a financial reparation they'll ask of you, but a punishment that they'll demand publicly. I don't need to remind Your Majesty of all the disastrous consequences which might result."

"You're too kind," muttered Boris, becoming more and more aware of the wasp's nest in which he'd put himself.

Then, he added, "You said there was another way to get out of it."

"Indeed, sire."

"What is it?"

"I daren't declare it to Your Majesty."

"Why?"

"Because I'm afraid that he'll refuse it with indignation."

"We'll see... tell me anyway."

"Sire, I'll be brutal."

"Right now, that suits me."

"If you wanted to avoid a scandal, which could have dangerous repercussions not just in France but further and particularly in Sokovia, Mademoiselle Gardannes must disappear."

"What do you mean, disappear?"

"Sire, I think that you understood me."

"You want to take her out?"

"I don't think we have to go quite that far."

"Then I don't understand."

"I'll develop my idea for Your Majesty."

"Develop, my friend, develop away, but hurry, because we need to act fast and take a decision before that ferocious child wakes up."

"May Your Majesty be assured," affirmed Arak, "that Mako is watching over her and he knows to prevent her from speaking, in the event where she's capable of doing so."

"I'm listening," said the king, letting himself drop, overwhelmed, into an armchair.

"Sire," continued the policeman, "in Sokovia there stands a fortress, which served for many years as a gaol for prisoners convicted of political crimes."

"Fortress Saint-Paul," the king said with a nod.

"These days it still houses some of those wretches, who, for crimes of sedition, have been condemned to lifelong imprisonment. This Sokovian Bastille is not just sheltered against any attack, but it fears no indiscretion. No one has ever succeeded in reaching those detained there, or even to communicate with them. All eventualities are foreseen: it takes the operation of just one secret mechanism for the whole fortress to explode, along with everyone inside.

"I must say that up to now, we've not needed that radical method and, given the excellent morale of Your Majesty's subjects, it's almost certain that such an eventuality will never arise.

"My idea would be to take the young woman there and lock her in that State prison. In that fashion, His Majesty would not have to reproach himself for having killed the unfortunate; but he would be forever beyond suspicion and, as a result, he would avoid the attacks which, if the scandal became public, would surely be directed against his person."

Boris, who had listened to his chief of police very carefully, replied nervously, "It's clear this system has merit and I assure you that, for my part, I don't intend to sacrifice the life of this little one towards whom, despite her obstinate resistance, I retain very ardent feelings.

"But several problems present themselves. This is the first: when the family realises she's not coming back, and discover that the so-called Roméro Levitz doesn't exist any more than the clinic of which he claimed to be the director, they'll call for an investigation.

"As you weren't disguised, and appeared to these people

as yourself, you'll be easily recognised, and if the French police ever get their hands on you, we'll soon be rumbled."

"Your Majesty will permit me to respond to the objection that he raises?"

"I ask nothing less."

"Sire," declared Arad, "you must have noticed that I was the opposite of other policemen. Most of the time, when a detective enters the fray, he feels the need to disguise himself and to transform his appearance completely. I do the opposite.

"When I'm resting, I disguise myself in various ways. It's by far the best way to escape those who might have an interest in finding me."

"Indeed," Boris said with an approving nod, "that's an ingenious approach."

"That's why," Arad concluded, "Your Majesty has seen me appear as different people."

"I see."

"So, when I've been notified of Your Majesty's intentions, I'll ask your permission to vanish for a while, and I'll return dressed as a gentleman with a moustache and sideburns in the Hungarian style, not bushy as in the past, but cut close, following the principles of modern hairstyling.

"As a consequence, I defy the most watchful French detective, even the one going by the famous name of Chantecoq, celebrated throughout the world as the greatest of us all, to find the man who fetched Mademoiselle Gardannes from her mother's house and brought her here."

And in a tone which, gradually, had regained its full assurance, Arad added, "Now, is Your Majesty persuaded?"

Boris replied, "I'm so much more so because up to now you have done me great service and averted many problems.

But that wasn't the only objection I had to offer. How would you manage, for example, to take Francine to Sokovia?"

"Majesty, that's a police matter, whose success I guarantee you."

"I know you're capable of doing what you promise; but I'm still curious to know the details."

"Sire, you're going to be satisfied. Your Majesty knows that in this house there's a secret apartment, known only to Mako and I. We'll take Mademoiselle Gardannes to this apartment; I'll care for her and that will be so much easier for me as I undertook, long ago, quite advanced medical studies. When I judge her well enough to take on such a long voyage, I'll leave with her in a specially arranged car where she'll have every comfort."

"Do you imagine that Francine will allow herself to be taken like that? No, my poor Arad. As soon as she's in the car, however well-adapted it may be, she'll let out terrifying screams. And at every stop - because you don't intend, I assume, to make this journey in one go - she won't hesitate to reveal her identity."

"Sire, I've foreseen everything. Before leaving, I'll make Mademoiselle Gardannes take a fresh sedative, which will plunge her into a deep sleep, capable of lasting close to a week. In the adapted car, which has already served me through various adventures, she'll be hidden in such a way that no one, even the driver, will notice her presence.

"Instead of getting out each evening into hotels, we'll stop during the day to rest, and drive throughout the night. I intend to arrive in Sokovia in fewer than five days.

"Permit me to finish by affirming to Your Majesty that I take full responsibility and that, should I fail, I would go myself to become a prisoner in the Saint-Paul fortress."

Boris thought for a few moments.

Certainly, this plan appeared rather dreamy, rather adventurous, but he had complete faith in the man in whom he had placed the difficult function of head of his secret police and he had, in any case, in many previous circumstances, shown that this faith was well placed.

So he replied, "Very well, it's agreed. Go ahead, just as you just told me; I believe, indeed, it's the only way for me to get out of this."

With a satisfied expression, Arad said, "In this fashion, Your Majesty won't lose hope of one day becoming this recalcitrant child's master: the four walls of a prison defeat the most obstinate resistance, especially when the captive knows she need say only a single word to obtain her liberty and see herself provided with all that a woman's ambition, pride and vanity could desire."

"Arad," said the amorous ogre, "I knew you were a first rate detective; but I didn't know you were such a profound psychologist. Your last argument is, indeed, decisive. It goes without saying that if, thanks to you, not only do I escape the bother that this adventure could cause, but if I also still manage to attain the goal that you know, I'll grant you the reward you've wanted for so long, and which I was reserving for the day of your retirement: the title of baron, with an endowment, which will permit you to cut a fine figure at court, in the fields and about the town."

"Sire," cried the policeman, carried away with joy, "I don't know how I can express my gratitude! How could I not be, body and soul, profoundly attached to Your Majesty, when you show me such unparalleled generosity!"

The king replied, "We're in agreement, then. Go back to this little one; take her, Mako and yourself, to the secret apartment; then make sure none of the servants are aware of anything.

"If you think that one of them has wind of the business, don't hesitate: great cures for great ills, doctor. One must always be wary of the valets, however devoted they appear. There's no need to worry about people of no importance. I needn't say more. As you just said, you were a doctor, or almost. So you know it's easier to kill people than cure them. You understand, don't you?"

"Yes, sire, it's not the first time it will have fallen to me to rid Your Majesty's path of certain sharp pebbles or brambles, or nettles which could hamper your passage."

"Very good, very good," said Boris who, to assure his security or even just indulge his whims, was capable of turning a blind eye to any crime, even taking the initiative if need be.

Realising the meeting was over, Arad gave a deep bow before his king, who deigned to wave a benevolent hand to him.

After having left the bedroom by the small door through which he had entered, he went back to the lounge to rejoin his colleague, Mako, who had stayed on guard with Francine.

She had not yet shown any signs of waking.

In a few words, Arad told his colleague about the agreement between Boris and himself.

Mako nodded his approval He was, indeed, extremely devoted to Arad, who he considered and respected as a leader.

Anyway, Arad held him by the most dubious bonds and could, with a single word, not only shatter his livelihood, but send him to the prison he had managed to evade in a shady business, so assuring himself, better than by any other means, the man's obedient loyalty.

He, in any case, wasn't lacking in intelligence, or finesse, and he complimented very well he who had made himself, by

72

default, his protector.

Mako, after listening to Arad, said, "Now, there's only one thing to do, that's to take this young lady to the secret apartment."

They went to grab her when, suddenly, a door opened with a bang, revealing a tall woman, tanned, with burning eyes, purple lips, flaring nostrils, and who, draped in a dark cloak, seemed to incarnate, in every sense of the word, that which the Americans call a 'vamp', the first syllable of the French word 'vampire'.

She was indeed troubling to the utmost. Of splendid beauty, and incomparable distinction, with a wilful chin and forehead, she seemed born to command, or rather to reign.

This woman was none other than Duchess Barbara de Castrovillari, official mistress of Boris I, King of Sokovia.

She was silent for a moment, fixed on the spot, darting her fiery gaze on the inanimate girl lying on the floor.

While the policemen, literally transfixed by this unexpected apparition, exchanged a keenly worried glance, she stepped forward and said in an authoritative metallic voice, "Who's this woman?"

Arad and Mako hesitated to respond.

The duchess continued. "I don't know why I'm asking. It's another of those little things you've brought, vile lackeys that you are, into your king's harem, or rather hunting grounds."

She approached and said, "She's dead!"

"No, duchess," replied Arad, "only injured."

"How did that happen?" Barbara asked.

"Madame," replied the chief of police, "we're not worthy to answer you. His Majesty alone…"

"Indeed," cut in the Duchess de Castrovillari, "I wonder why I'm lowering myself to address words to individuals of your calibre. I'm going to find the king."

She took a few steps towards a door which led to His Majesty's room, but the door opened before she could reach it, and Boris appeared on the threshold.

On seeing his favourite, he couldn't repress a shudder, and without even giving him time to utter a word, Barbara launched herself towards him and asked in a bitter and decisive tone, "Who is this woman?"

The king immediately realised a storm was about to break over his head and he said, "Please come to my room, my dear duchess, I'm going to explain everything to you."

"So be it," accepted Barbara.

And while the sovereign made way for her, she entered the room.

The king had time to send a signal to Arad, who responded with an equally swift wink of acknowledgement.

Closing the door, he went towards his mistress who, in a single movement, having let her cloak fall on the carpet, was standing, superb, sculpted, shaking with barely-contained rage, before Boris, who was saying to himself, "What's this shrew going to say this time?"

Her lips pinched, her nostrils flaring, and her eyes shining with growing fury, the Duchess de Castrovillari began.

"You must be wondering why I'm here?"

"Yes," retorted the king, "I left you this afternoon around four o'clock, and though we were in complete harmony, I wasn't expecting you to feel the need to see me again so soon. For myself, I'm charmed, and…"

The duchess thundered, "No need to play games with me. You're not charmed at all; instead you're deeply put out that I surprised your two agents, your two damned souls, at the side of a gravely ill young girl who seems to me to be grievously injured."

"Let's see, let's see," Boris tried to calm her down. "I wonder why you're attaching such importance to an incident which really isn't that serious."

"I'm used to your infidelities," replied Barbara. "I resigned myself to them long ago. You love me no longer, I love you no longer. But don't forget there remains between us a bond far more powerful than that of love: self-interest!

"I'm not insisting, you've made me well aware of that. Very well! It's in the name of self-interest that I'm here, this evening, not to ask you to account for yourself, because you can cheat on me with all the girls and even all the young girls that you fancy, but there's one thing I forbid you from committing: that's to compromise your prestige and, who knows, perhaps even risk your crown in these adventures."

"So, you know, then."

"Yes, I know."

"Did Arad talk about it?"

"He's incapable of doing so. He's too much your damned soul to ever become mine." And she uttered this most atrocious phrase, "One can't live in two hells at once.

"However, there's no need to waste our time in ridiculous preliminaries. Let's get straight to the point. You have your police, Monsieur King, and I have mine. I learned that, for some time, you've been unreasonably hung up on a young girl who belongs to an honourable family and who is engaged to a young engineer. I wanted to see her... I've seen her...

"As much as those ladies of the music-hall, those underworld creatures, and all those sellers of love who ply their trade in Paris have left me indifferent, as much as I understood that, if, unfortunately for her, that young Francine Gardannes fell into your hands, you risked finding in her precisely the mistress that I forbade you, that's to say one to which you'd become attached, one which you can no longer get over and who, spineless and feeble as you are, couldn't fail to swiftly discover how to pull on the strings of the puppet that you are.

"Those strings, I intend that none but I should have the right to make use of! What happened here this evening? I guess it… you wanted, with all the delicacy that characterises you, to take that young girl by force, after having drawn her into an ambush concocted by your Arad.

"The girl defended herself and, brutal as you are, you struck her with abominable violence."

Boris, who was forcing himself to keep calm, replied, "Duchess, I'll stop you there. Your perspicacity is way off, at least on that last point. I did not employ any violence against that lady, it was she who was stupid enough to fling herself through the window because, I may as well admit it, I was holding her a little too closely. She was lucky enough to survive, and you see that I'm rather relieved."

In a strange tone, Barbara replied, "You're that attached to her?"

"No, but in the end, I won't pretend that it would have been disagreeable and even tiresome for me to be forced to get rid of her corpse."

"And yet," hissed the Duchess de Castrovillari, "that's what you're going to have to do."

"What are you saying?" cried the king.

"Would you prefer to send her back home to her family?"

"There's no question of that," retorted Boris.

"So, what are you going to do with her?"

The king, on whom the mistress was exerting some dominance, which must have been limitless, replied, "Send her to Sokovia and have her locked up in Saint-Paul

Fortress."

"What a wild yarn you're spinning me!"

"It's not a wild yarn, it's a very serious plan, indeed."

"Born no doubt from Monsieur Arad's imagination."

With a semblance of authority, Boris declared, "Arad is a servant in whom I can trust entirely. Since he's engaged himself to carry out the plan that he indeed suggested to me, I've no reason to forbid him, so much more so, as you'll acknowledge yourself, as we don't exactly have a great deal of choice."

"My choice has been made," decided Barbara, with an edge to her voice that made the amorous ogre shudder.

In a slightly trembling voice, he asked, "What is it?"

"That young girl must die."

"Oh no!" Boris protested. "You want to make a murderer of me, then?"

The duchess burst into a peal of dreadful laughter. "My word, anyone would think you were a beginner at it. Oh! My dear, if we had to count up all the bodies..."

"Silence, silence!" cried the sovereign in a strangled voice.

"If you want me to be silent," replied the mistress, whose rage had now fallen away, "you'll carry out my will."

"Your will?"

"Yes, you're going to transport that young girl at once to the secret apartment..."

"What, you knew about that?"

"Yes, yes, I know, I know... and many more things besides," declared Barbara with a smile full of innuendo and threats. "So you're going to take your victim where I tell you. Then, leave me alone with her. I'll take care of everything. Is that understood?"

The king was silent. Despite everything, he was still

struggling with his conscience, which had awoken for a moment, but, on the other hand, dominated by the gaze with which his mistress was blasting him, trembling at the reprisals that she wouldn't hesitate to take against him, he was afraid at the thought of the irreparable disaster into which his honour and his crown risked sinking.

So he said, "Very well! So be it, it will be done according to your desire."

And he sank down on to a divan under the weight of his cowardice, his shame, his infamy.

Barbara contemplated him with a contemptuous expression, which was bordering on disgust, and she went back to the lounge.

It was empty.

She started in rage and snarled between her teeth, "Very funny! Trying to play games with me."

Returning to the king's room, she said to him, "The young girl is no longer in the lounge. Your minions must have taken her up to the secret apartment. You're going to take me there at once, you're going to send them away, and then you'll leave, because I don't need anyone, and much less them and you, to do you the service for which you'll thank me one day."

Boris stumbled to his feet, painfully.

He went out into a corridor which ended in a plain panel and which, according to the house's architecture, ought to form a supporting wall.

Once there, he must have pressed an invisible spring, because the panel swung open, revealing a gap large enough to allow the king and his mistress to pass through.

While the panel was closing behind them, they crossed a deliciously decorated hallway, in the Directoire style.

Boris went straight to a door that he opened. In a

luxurious room, in the same style as the hallway, Francine was lying on a bed, flanked by the two agents, who seemed to mount a vigilant guard over the young girl.

Barbara approached the bed, while the king ordered, "Arad, Mako, withdraw!"

Arad replied, "Sire, I must announce to Your Majesty that Mako and I are watching over a dead body. Mademoiselle Gardannes indeed expired, not two minutes ago."

The king gave a squeal of emotion. The Duchess de Castrovillari cried, "There's an event which will simplify things, if indeed it's true."

Boris turned an interrogative gaze on his chief of police. He dared to reply, "The duchess believes us capable of such trickery, then?"

"Perfectly," replied the Italian.

Arad declared, "Madame can approach. She'll observe that we spoke the truth."

"So as to be certain of it," emphasised the mistress, "I mean to pour a drop of cyanide in the corner of this woman's eye. That way, I'll be sure she can't be resuscitated."

To Boris's sharp astonishment, Arad bowed, saying, "May your will be done, duchess, but unfortunately I don't have any cyanide on my person. It may be procured only by medical prescription."

Disdainfully, Barbara replied, "Monsieur chief of secret police, if the agents you charged with watching me had truly and conscientiously carried out their mission, they would have told you that the Duchess de Castrovillari always carries on her person a flask filled with this lethal poison, as well as a dropper, which can be useful on occasion. Needless to say, this evening, I'm equipped with that flask and dropper."

"Then," replied Arad, "I have nothing more to say."

While the duchess took from her bag a case which

contained the objects she had described, the monarch shot a worried glance towards Arad, who remained impassive.

With diabolical sang-froid, the duchess filled her dropper with the liquid in the flask and, approaching Francine whose face was giving every impression of death, she dropped in each of the unfortunate girl's half-open and glazed eyes, a drop of that unforgiving poison.

Boris, Arad, and Mako remained impassive.

The king's mistress, calmly, as though treating an ill patient, stowed the flask and dropper back in her bag.

Then she said simply, turning towards the two agents, "Take care of getting rid of this body, that's your business and doesn't concern me."

And turning towards the sovereign, towards the murderer king who, worthy of his accomplice, had witnessed this abominable scene impassively, she added, "Now, I need a word with you."

"Come," Boris said simply, taking Barbara to his room.

As soon as they were alone, the Duchess de Castrovillari attacked with authority.

"This time, I agree to forgive you; but let this ridiculous story, which could have ended so badly for you, be the last. I'm absolutely counting on it, and above all don't forget that henceforth, I intend to have absolute control over your passing fancies; if not, I'll find myself obliged to declare a war on you from which, it's certain, you would not emerge victorious."

"My dear love," declared the king of Sokovia, "you know the attachment that I have to you... It's therefore superfluous to add that I'll strive to avoid the slightest element of conflict between us."

"I dare to hope that you'll keep your word. Now, I only wish that the end of your night turns out better than the beginning."

"Are you leaving me already?" Boris cried, with a somewhat forced note of gallantry.

"I wouldn't want to inconvenience you any longer with my presence," retorted the mistress.

The Count d'Esseck protested, "How can you talk like that? You know very well that I greatly appreciate the pleasure of spending time with you, so much more so as, this evening, you've never been so beautiful."

"I beg you, spare me those compliments of which you think so little and for which I no longer care. We're no longer lovers, but simply associates."

And as though she thought she saw desire spark in the amorous ogre's eyes, she said, "Don't force me to remind you what has been agreed between us."

"There have been a great many things agreed between us," stressed the king, with a sad smile.

"I know," said the duchess, "and be sure that I've not forgotten any of the articles of our contract. But there's one, especially, to which I hold more than all the others: that there must only exist between us… let's say links… I daren't say of friendship, camaraderie seems to me to be a no less improper term… let's say links of *interest* and we'll be along the right lines."

The sovereign replied, "If you only knew how painful it is to hear you talk like that."

"Why?" the beautiful Italian asked.

"Because I've maintained a very deep attachment to you…"

Barbara retorted, "Which doesn't stop you betraying me with the first woman who comes along!"

Boris made a gesture of protest.

"Oh! Calm down," said the Duchess of Castrovillari, "I'm not going to make a jealous scene for you. I'll simply say that I don't want to have the leftovers from those scheduled courtesans, from those stupid bourgeois girls, whom it pleases you to make your ephemeral favourites. Let's leave it there, I sense that we'll begin to disagree, and I prefer never to anger myself needlessly. I have an important lunch tomorrow and I want to be on form. Goodbye, sire…"

This time, Boris made no attempt to call her back.

When she had left through the door which led to the great lounge, the King of Sokovia began to murmur, "What a nuisance! Ah! If only I'd never committed the crazy act of sharing State secrets with her and, above all, letting myself be robbed of the documents whose publication could provoke catastrophes, I'd have sent her with pleasure to sand the chianti in her Ravenna villa.

"And to think I don't even have the recourse of bumping her off, since she took her precautions, and that in case of death the blackmail with which she menaces me in life would burst out fully. There's nothing to do but bite my tongue. But how clumsy I was! How could I have pushed that child to throw herself from the window? She was kind… it's a shame!"

And that was the entire funereal oratory that the amorous ogre granted she that one hour previously he was pursuing with his odious assiduity.

5 CHANTECOQ

We'll refrain from describing Madame Gardannes's emotional state, when she didn't see her daughter return home.

At first, she was only relatively worried. She said to herself, "Francine must have wanted to stay by her fiancé's bedside. What surprises me is that she didn't telephone to let me know. Doubtless the situation was more serious than they told us! And she'll have lost her head…"

At length, around five o'clock in the morning, she looked in the directory for the number for the clinic on Boulevard Delessert.

To her great surprise, she couldn't find it.

She called "Directory Enquiries" to ask for an explanation where she ended up learning, not without some difficulty, that the clinic didn't feature among the telephone system's subscribers.

"Well that's strange!" she said to herself. "Such an important house, where they must have many sick people, not having a telephone…"

At eight o'clock in the morning, unable to wait any longer, she called her chambermaid and ordered her to take a taxi to the address indicated.

One hour later, the maid returned, declaring that the clinic didn't exist.

Gripped by unspeakable anguish, Madame Gardannes had an intuition that her daughter must have been lured into an ambush. And yet, she knew of no enemies.

Francine, for her part, only seemed to attract the warmest generosity.

The jealousy of a supplanted lover? Already, several times, the young artist had received marriage proposals, even rather flattering ones, but, among those who had declared themselves, Madame Gardannes was certain there were none capable of such cowardice.

What to do?

She was too frail to go out, to telephone the police herself. Wouldn't it be better to await Robert Santenois's return before taking the next steps?

And would Robert Santenois himself return? He hadn't sent any telegram explaining the extension of his trip to Rouen.

Who knew if he too hadn't been subject to an attack?

The poor mother felt she was going mad. Her chambermaid, who was very devoted to her, tried hard to console her; she didn't manage it.

In the end, unable to wait any longer, Madame Gardannes was about to send for one of her cousins, who lived on Boulevard de Clichy and with whom she maintained an ancient and loyal friendship, when the hallway bell rang.

Madame Gardannes started in shock. Quickly, her maid went to open the door: it was Robert Santenois who, appearing tired, his features drawn, presented himself, saying, "I'm sorry. How are the ladies?"

The chambermaid didn't know what to say; she didn't dare tell the young engineer the sad truth.

She replied simply, "Madame Gardannes had a very bad night."

"And Mademoiselle Francine?" Santenois asked.

The maid bit her lip, and two tears appeared in her eyes.

Robert cried, "Something must have happened tonight, something very serious. Mariette, you're a brave girl, I know you have a good heart. Tell me honestly. Tell me the truth, the whole truth."

Mariette, wiping her eyes, replied, "It would be better if you spoke to Madame…"

And she led Robert, breathless with anxiety, into the lounge.

Madame Gardannes, lying on a divan, cried out, holding out her arms to him, "Robert, it's you. And Francine? She's not with you?"

"No, madame," replied Santenois.

"Then where is she?"

"What?" the engineer was astonished. "Isn't she here?"

"No," sobbed the distraught mother. "She's not here."

"What's become of her? What happened?" the young engineer asked feverishly.

Madame Gardannes explained.

"Last night, Francine and I were waiting for you. We were starting to worry that you were late, as you're always so punctual, when there was a knock at the door. Mariette told us that a Monsieur Levitz, director of a clinic on Boulevard

Delessert, wanted to speak to us about an urgent matter.

"We received him at once, because we feared that you'd had an accident.

"Monsieur Levitz, who seemed to be an extremely honourable man, even distinguished, told us with great tact that on returning from Rouen, you'd been afflicted, on the train, with an attack of acute appendicitis and that, as soon as you arrived back in Paris, you had to be taken with all haste to the clinic of which he was the director.

"He added that it was essential to operate on you right away and that you were asking Francine to come at once to be with you. We were completely unsuspecting. I repeat, this man introduced himself perfectly and inspired real confidence in us.

"He offered to take Francine in his car. My daughter accepted, she left with him. I've not seen her since! I learned that there is no clinic on Boulevard Delessert. Isn't that dreadful?"

Grasping her future son-in-law's hand, she cried, "You'll help me get her back, won't you, that poor darling? We can't leave her like this. Into whose clutches has she fallen? What have they done with her? Oh! It's frightful, Robert, it's frightful!"

Santenois replied, with a voice full of sorrow. "There's no doubt Francine has been lured into a trap, but by whom?"

Madame Gardannes said, "I was just wondering that myself."

"We must get on her trail at once, without losing a single minute."

"The best thing," said the mother, "would be to make a report to the police at once."

"No, madame," said the young man, "at the moment the police have so much on their hands, that all their best inspectors will be up to their eyes in work, and it would be better, I think, if we want to move fast, to contact a private detective agency, to whom we'd promise a hefty fee, so as to stimulate their zeal. We'd get a much swifter result than if we used the normal channels."

"Do you know one of these agencies?" Madame Gardannes asked.

"No, but I've heard much talk of one private detective called Chantecoq, who is renowned as the most skillful and honest detective of our age.

"If he agrees to look for Francine, I'm convinced he'll find her, and as soon as possible. This man, indeed, since he founded a private detective agency, has achieved some real marvels. You've certainly heard of his exploits during the War, in the course of which he carried out an extraordinary hunt for enemy spies…"

"I remember now," declared Madame Gardannes, "and some time ago, I happened to find myself, while visiting my cousin Bérot, in the company of his daughter and his son-in-law."

"Still more recently," continued Robert, "he's found the means, in several successive and sensational cases, of which the press has spoken a great deal, that's to say *The Mystery of the Blue Train*, *The Haunted House of the Quiberon Peninsula*, *The Aviator's Crime*, *Zapata*, to achieve a glory I can describe only as global."

"Would he bother himself with us?" asked the mother anxiously.

"Why not? The case is worth the trouble. Anyway, let's try. If he does refuse, it will be time to speak to one of his colleagues or to pursue justice directly.

"I'm going to go to Chantecoq at once. Will you permit

me to look up his address in your telephone directory?"

"Please do…"

Santenois grabbed the volume, leafed through it, and wrote, on a page in his pocket notebook, the famous bloodhound's address and telephone number.

Then he turned back to Madame Gardannes and said, "I beg you, try to calm yourself. I promise I'll do whatever it takes to bring your child home. If she is all your happiness, she is also all mine and, without her, life would be impossible for me. I love her so much."

"And she loves you so much too," said Madame Gardannes, clasping the young engineer in her arms, as he fought to hold back his tears.

***

In a very light studio, furnished with taste, and which more closely resembled an artist's workshop than a detective's office, two men were present. One was none other than Robert Santenois who, sitting on a chair, opposite a desk, behind which Chantecoq himself was installed, had just brought that great detective up to date with his fiancée's mysterious abduction during the course of the previous night.

Chantecoq was one of those men whose age is impossible to define precisely.

All that could be said of him was that he must have been between forty and fifty years old.

Dressed with a sober elegance, and with a classical profile, eyes that were loyal, sharp, and penetrating, and a smile that was without irony, he inspired confidence at first sight.

"Dear monsieur," he said in a voice that was very compassionate, and which he knew, through friendly inflections, how to attenuate the naturally metallic sparkle, "you can congratulate yourself, as you are so keen for me to look into this case, yes, you can congratulate yourself on being very lucky, because I have a good month ahead of me at the moment.

"I was preparing, indeed, to go to the Midi[9], to visit one of my friends. But my friend will wait. Duty comes first, and I consider it a duty to be of service to you.

"I don't know you, monsieur; I have no information about you, I know only what you've told me. I know this sad story we're discussing only from what you've told me. Well! Despite that, I don't hesitate to tell you: you can count on me… and you know why? Because, gifted as I am with a certain flair, I'll even call it a flair for certainty - that's my single pretension - I perceive in you, not just an honest man, but a man nobly in love with a young woman who is truly worthy of him.

"I needn't say any more about that, any more than we'll speak of the conditions on which I'm granting you my assistance. It's one pleasant aspect of my profession, to be able to indulge my philanthropy from time to time, especially when it's a matter of two lovers separated brutally and whose shattered happiness must be rebuilt."

Very moved, the young engineer said, "I don't know, Monsieur Chantecoq, how to express my gratitude to you. I have often heard your praises sung, but I realise they fell short of the truth."

"Don't say another word," the king of detectives advised him. "You'd make me blush, and that's a tint that I permit to grace my cheeks only when I'm obliged to disguise myself, which, by the way, happens quite often, as you'll certainly

---

[9] Broadly, the South of France.

have the opportunity to discover.

"Now, I'm going to ask you for some information I'll need to start my investigations at once."

Santenois replied, "Interrogate me, I'll answer."

"You just told me that, if you weren't able to return on the train from Rouen last night, it was because, after drinking a cup of tea in a cafe during the afternoon, you felt overcome by such torpor that you were unable to move and you had to be taken to the hotel where you stayed."

"That's right, Monsieur Chantecoq."

"At what time did you wake up?"

"In the night, at four o'clock in the morning. I had a heavy head, and a bitter taste in my mouth."

"It's certain," the great bloodhound concluded, "that you had been sedated, or rather knocked out, with the help of a narcotic."

"That's just what I think," said the young engineer.

"Then what did you do?"

"I took the first train to Paris; I went straight to Madame Gardannes, because I thought she must be extremely worried and that she might think I'd had an accident.

"It's then that I learned, from the mouth of my future mother-in-law, that my fiancée had vanished in the circumstances I described."

"This then is very clear," concluded the king of detectives. "To prevent your return to Paris, which would have demolished the plot against Mademoiselle Gardannes, you were drugged. So this is without doubt a kidnapping case. That's already helpful. Now, when one is called to investigate such a case, it's important to know its cause from the outset. Among your relations or those of Mademoiselle Gardannes, are any people capable of committing such infamy?"

"No, monsieur," the young engineer replied categorically. "That is, however, the first question I posed myself and, despite all my efforts, I find it impossible to suspect anyone."

"This is clear," the detective said appreciatively, listening to his visitor without taking any notes.

"Another thing," he continued. "Couldn't Mademoiselle Gardannes have recently made the acquaintance of any suspicious or shady people? I don't know her, I'm sure she's the most honourable young girl and the most worthy of all respect."

"Indeed, Monsieur Chantecoq."

"But she is an artist, and a painter. Necessarily, she is obliged to move in certain circles…"

"No," Robert interrupted. "Mademoiselle Gardannes has always had, instead, an instinctive suspicion of people she doesn't know; and she's always carefully avoided frequenting places of which she's not absolutely sure. She's an artist, indeed, and a very beautiful artist. But she's remained the true young girl of the world in every sense of the word, not at all modern, and even condemning the audacious steps taken by young people who ought to be called upon, by the rank they hold in the world, to set a good example to all."

"Congratulations," replied Chantecoq, "on being able to win the heart of such an accomplished young woman. Every day I notice her type grows rarer, thanks to the snobbery-impregnated education given by unaware parents or, rather, that they allow to be given to their children. But let's get back to the point. Do you have a portrait of your fiancée with you?"

"I do, monsieur."

"Can you give it to me?"

"Gladly."

Robert took a wallet from his jacket pocket from which he took a photo. He gave it to the detective with a hand that trembled slightly with emotion.

Chantecoq looked at it carefully; then he said, "She's adorably pretty."

"Isn't she though, monsieur?"

"She must be extremely good and tender."

"You're an admirable judge of character. I see, monsieur, you were right when you mentioned your flair."

"Oh!" Chantecoq replied, "You don't need much flair to perceive what an exquisite soul is contained within this equally exquisite envelope. She's one of the prettiest young girls I've ever seen."

He thought for a moment, then continued. "Would it be too much to ask to keep this portrait?"

"Monsieur Chantecoq, I understand how necessary it is, and I have others."

While continuing to study the portrait, the great bloodhound said, "There's nothing extraordinary in Mademoiselle Gardannes having been the object of ardent longing. I don't think that she's been abducted by those dreadful traffickers who generally target a less lofty category of society, and abuse the candour of young girls recently arrived in Paris from the depths of their province. I'm already certain that it's in a completely different direction that we're going to aim our search."

Chantecoq was quiet for a moment. Santenois realised he ought to respect his silence.

At once, the famous detective had exercised a remarkable influence over him, which he always knew, regardless of the circumstances, how to use wisely.

This silence didn't last long however. The great private

policeman was one of those who know how to think fast and take prompt decisions.

And he asked, "Tell me, monsieur, I beg your pardon for intruding on your private life, and that of your fiancée like this, but it's essential for me. It's said with good reason that sometimes all you need is one spark to start a great fire; sometimes all it takes is one tiny scrap of an idea, a fragile point of departure, to lead you to the truth.

"That's why I'm asking you if, recently, you haven't met on your travels someone who, without you being aware of it, may have had shady intentions with regard to Mademoiselle Gardannes."

"No," replied the young engineer, "I don't remember."

"Search your memory, because I'm certain I've put my finger on the key to this case."

Santenois began to reflect, then, suddenly, he cried out, "I remember now. We did meet, quite by chance, a foreign gentleman, who had knocked down a young worker with his car.

"As it wasn't the driver's fault, my fiancée and I offered to act as witnesses for this gentleman. The crowd was beginning to abuse him. This gentleman accepted. I offered to guide him to the hospital where he took the injured man. He thanked me effusively, as well as Mademoiselle Gardannes, but we've not seen him since and we've heard nothing more about him."

"Did he give you his name?" the king of detectives asked.

Santenois responded, "He did better than that: he gave me his card, I must even have kept it in my wallet."

Robert looked for, and indeed found, the card in question, and gave it to Chantecoq.

He took it, and had hardly glanced at it when he started with surprise.

93

"The Count d'Esseck," he cried, "what, he was the hero of this car accident?"

"Exactly, Monsieur Chantecoq."

"You're sure of that?"

"Absolutely sure."

"But then," replied the king of detectives, "it's he who…"

He stopped himself, and cleared his throat. "Give me a description of this man."

"Tall, distinguished, a little distant, his hair slightly greying, cut in the American style."

"Didn't he have a faint scar near his right eye?"

"You know him, then?"

"Answer my question first, dear monsieur."

"Yes, I did notice such a scar."

"Then," concluded the great bloodhound, "there's no doubt, it was he who kidnapped or who arranged the kidnapping of your fiancée."

"Monsieur Chantecoq," exclaimed Santenois, stupefied, "how can you be so certain so quickly?"

"Because the man in question is no beginner, and this isn't the first time he's attacked a woman in such a brutal fashion. Up to now, he respected young girls; but now I see he has put no brakes on his base desires. I repeat, this man is the culprit."

Santenois cried, "Monsieur Chantecoq, I was truly inspired in coming to find you, since the fact alone of knowing the culprit is going to permit you to save his victim."

"I intend to," cried the king of detectives. "I wouldn't want to bring despair to your soul, far from it, first because I'm already rather fond of you, and being of an optimistic character, I've always observed that the best way to achieve victory is to believe in it, even if the battle has not yet been joined. I believe I can promise, without fear of error, that your fiancée will soon be found."

"Monsieur, I'll be eternally grateful."

"Now," declared the bloodhound, "I have a duty to warn you that we're going to encounter some extremely serious difficulties. You have no idea who the Count d'Esseck really is."

"Indeed, Monsieur Chantecoq."

"Well! He's none other than Boris I, King of Sokovia, who comes every year, sheltering behind his borrowed name, to enjoy Paris incognito in what had been until now only degrading debauchery, and which now is more than a crime. You acted very wisely, in not going to the state police, because, due to orders from on high, they would have been obliged, to their keen regret, I'm sure, to withhold any useful assistance from you.

"The King of Sokovia is, indeed, an ally and creditor to France. Orders have been given, I know this from a firm source, not only to turn a blind eye to his misdemeanours, but further to stifle any scandal he provokes."

The young engineer looked afraid. "Monsieur Chantecoq, it will be impossible to reach him…"

"Oh! For me, my dear monsieur," retorted the fine bloodhound with an ironic smile, "that's not the case at all. I don't take orders from anyone, I act in line with my conscience, at total liberty and taking full responsibility.

"What do we want, first and foremost? To recover Mademoiselle Gardannes. That's it. There's no need to provoke a scandal which could turn out badly, not just for she whom you're trying to save, but also for yourself. Don't ask me to talk about this for too long. You're an extremely intelligent lad, you understand me, that's enough. Let's pass to the practical side of the case and not get bogged down in thoughts of future reprisals. A day will come when the Sokovian people, I'm quite sure, will inflict on their unworthy monarch the penalty that his infamy deserves."

Santenois cried, "Your language, Monsieur Chantecoq, is that of reason and wisdom themselves. I can only tell you one thing: I approve of your reasoning entirely and I'm placing myself at your complete disposal, in case you need me, at any time of day or night."

Chantecoq replied, "Thank you, because it could well be that given the struggle I'm going to be undertaking against this disgusting potentate, I may have need of your assistance."

"I grant it in advance."

And anxious to add to the hopes that the king of detectives had raised in him, the fiancé added, "What are you going to do, Monsieur Chantecoq?"

He replied in a tone that was full of benevolence. "You don't know me yet. If you did, you'd know that, when I've entered into action, I demand instantly to all those surrounding me, and even the people most interested in the success of the case in question, to have complete confidence in me, and never to ask me questions."

"Pardon me, Monsieur Chantecoq, if I was indiscreet. Be assured that in future I'll be on guard against that."

"You don't blame me for my frankness?"

"No, rather I thank you for it," affirmed Santenois as he stood up.

Chantecoq did the same.

They exchanged a cordial handshake. Then, the bloodhound said, "Where must I go, if I need to speak to you or to see you? It's bound to happen soon."

Robert gave the private detective a card with the address

of his factory and his private residence. "In the morning, I'm in the factory from nine o'clock until noon. Then I have lunch in a neighbouring restaurant, and I return to my office at two o'clock. I leave at seven o'clock in the evening. I dine again at the restaurant and return home at half past eight, if I'm not spending the evening with Madame Gardannes, whose address and telephone number are also here.

Chantecoq took a note of this last detail; then, staring into his client's eyes, he said, "Did you have something else to say to me, dear monsieur."

"Yes, Monsieur Chantecoq," replied the young engineer, "but I don't want to waste your time."

"You're not wasting anything, far from it…"

"Very well! Monsieur, I don't want to ask you any questions, but I'd like to ask your advice."

"Speak."

"Madame Gardannes, I hardly need tell you, finds herself, at this moment, in the most agonising position that could break any mother's heart; I would simply like to know what I ought to tell her."

Chantecoq asked, "Is Madame Gardannes a discreet woman?"

"Yes," replied Robert simply, "but I fear that, in the depths of her pain, she might let out, to a few of her friends, some confidences which could be repeated and risk paralysing your action."

"I'm very satisfied, monsieur, that you're talking to me about this," declared Chantecoq. "It proves that the great pain you're suffering hasn't blunted your understanding, or your reasoning.

"From what you've told me, there's no need to go into the details with Madame Gardannes. You can simply tell her

I've accepted to take on this case and that… or rather no, tell her that I've refused, because my time is taken up for several weeks at this point, but that I've given you the address of one of my colleagues who desires, for reasons that are personal and so as not to draw the abductor's attention on himself, to remain completely anonymous, and that he has made you give your word of honour not to reveal his name to a living soul.

"Obviously all that's a bit, even a lot, of a lie, but what can you do in police work? Especially when you're facing an adversary of King Boris's stature, you can't take too many precautions. If Madame Gardannes, as she won't fail to do, asks for your impressions of the detective, you can respond, without fear of fobbing her off with false illusions, that he has every hope of success.

"Then you'll certainly find the words, both prudent and necessary, to appease her immense chagrin, before which I respectfully bow."

"I must thank you again, Monsieur Chantecoq," said Robert Santenois. "Thanks to you, I'm going from here very reassured and full of confidence in the man that you are."

They exchanged another handshake. Chantecoq led his visitor into the hallway himself.

When he returned to his studio, another young man, who looked lively, alert, wide awake, his nose slightly turned up, with the appearance of a jockey deprived of his helmet or a clown stripped of his tinsel, was standing in front of his desk, holding numerous sheets in his hand.

"Ah, there you are, Météor!" exclaimed the king of detectives.

All those who have already made the acquaintance of Chantecoq and his secretary will have recognised in this newcomer, the great bloodhound's precious and alert collaborator, that he had given the nickname Météor, because, gifted with surprising agility, he appeared and disappeared as fast as thought.

At once, without giving his secretary time to respond, the policeman asked, "Well! You heard everything?"

"Yes, boss," replied Météor. "The proof is that I've taken, as usual, the complete stenography of the meeting that you just had with Monsieur Santenois, and I hope that this work, once written up, won't need, as they say, to be seen and expurgated by an honourable ecclesiastical court."

"Always the joker," said Chantecoq.

"Ah! Boss, you have to be. However, except for the respect that I owe you, I only follow your example. If there's ever been a man of good humour, it's you. Only, it's not at all the same thing: your own good humour, boss, it's in your mind. Mine… comes out through jokes."

Chantecoq concluded, "Which all proves that we're both blessed with very good health. You have to be, in our profession; and then, you see, we encounter such sadness, we experience such dramas, we witness scenes so dreadful, we receive confidences so painful, that, if we didn't evade that atmosphere as often as possible, we'd both have the blues. Now, you see, Météor, when a detective has the blues, he's worthless."

"How right you are, boss! And with you, life is good!"

Chantecoq replied, "Now, let's talk seriously. What do you make of this case?"

Météor replied, "First, boss, I think you're doing me a great honour by asking my opinion."

"Yes, of course I do, and then what?"

"I also think this King of Sokovia, this Boris I, is a disgusting individual."

"Yes, yes, that still goes without saying. But that's not

what I'm asking you. Do you agree with my affirmation that it was him who kidnapped that young girl?"

"Well, let's see, boss, that's a poke in the eye, and I don't know why you're asking me that."

"Simply because I don't pretend to be infallible."

"You're wrong, boss... you're more infallible still than the pope. Only, but, I don't want to say any more about it to you."

"Why?"

"Because I'm afraid of having, in your eyes, appeared not to make any progress."

"To the contrary, you're making progress every day, I'm the first to notice it, to compliment you on it, and to congratulate myself for it. So, speak..."

"Boss!"

"I'm going to pose you a question to which I order you to respond, because it will be the only way for me to get a sense of where your detective's education has reached."

Météor scratched his nose, not because he lacked ideas, but he was highly perplexed, so great was his fear of displeasing his master, to whom he had pledged boundless admiration.

And he thought, "So long as I don't say anything nonsensical, so long as I don't make a gaffe!"

Chantecoq, pretending to grow impatient, said, "Oh! My friend, let's see, hurry up, you're making me waste precious time."

Météor made up his mind.

"Boss, if it was a civilian, the case wouldn't be hard to pin down. You'd find the guy and you'd talk to him as you know how to talk to villains like him, and you'd sort it out in five seconds...

"Only, a king, that's not a bloke who handles himself like a sack of potatoes. You'll have to tie your tongue in knots several times before arguing with him, without taking into account that it's going to take some serious work even to approach him.

"That one in particular. I've heard it said he's always accompanied by two dirty snitches who are called, it appears, Baraque and Malikoko.

"There we are, what names! If I'm ever a godfather or if I ever have any kids, I'll choose different ones, right? When you hand out a name like that, you're bound to have crimes on your conscience!

"I know, boss, that two rascals like that are hardly likely to intimidate you and you'll quickly reduce them to dust... only, in this kind of story, it's not so much the men I fear as the things."

"What things?" asked Chantecoq.

"I'm going to tell you, boss. I'm not too badly read up on the works of père Dumas. They're exciting! What's amusing is that they're rousing! And then, above all, one feels that it's not history and that it's true all the same."

"Oh!" cried the king of detectives, "I wonder what the author of *The Three Musketeers* is going to bring to this adventure."

Météor replied, "Wait a bit, boss, you're going to see that he's not arriving like hair in the soup, quite the reverse. Because, it's thanks to him that, today, I know many things I didn't used to know and that, notably, kings, when they find themselves with people who are questioning them or trying to threaten them, ah... it's not for long: they have them poisoned without giving them time to say 'oof' or throw them into the dungeons from where, naturally, they never return.

"Well! Boss, since you asked me for my opinion, I'm going to give it to you. For me, these days, things haven't changed.

"You must have noticed better than I, since you always keep your eyes open, that in royal and imperial courts, and even in certain republics, there are from time to time some fellows or ladies who vanish without anyone ever knowing what became of them."

"So," said Chantecoq with a smile, as he enjoyed his secretary's flights of fancy greatly, especially when he had time to listen to them, "you believe there are dungeons in the Elysée?"

"I'm not going that far; because the Presidents of the Republic that we've had, from Grévy[10] to Monsieur Doumergue[11], are incapable even of killing a fly. Here we still have, whatever they say, a better type of men, even among politicians. Only, the thing is, I wouldn't say so much for Boris, and I wouldn't be astonished if there were in his house, where he resides under the name of Count d'Esseck, a few traps, perfectly capable of opening under the feet of those who had the misfortune to displease this crowned weirdo."

"In conclusion," replied Chantecoq, "you're not advising me to venture into that building."

"Oh, boss, I don't advise you to do anything at all, first, I wouldn't allow myself the liberty of doing so, and then, if you've got it in your head to tickle Boris under the chin, this evening or tomorrow, I know you far too well not to be sure that nothing would prevent you from doing so.

---

[10] Jules Grévy (1807-1891). President of the French Republic from 1879 to 1887. Great billiards player.
[11] Gaston Doumergue (1863-1937). President of the French Republic from 1924 to 1931. Once accidentally fell off a train.

"All I can tell you is that, in order to get out of such a wasp's-nest, you must be what you are: the ace of super aces, the king of detectives, the famous and immortal Chantecoq."

"No, no," said the great bloodhound, "it's not as complicated or as perilous as you think. It's enough to have some flair, intelligence, composure, and one always sorts things out."

"Yes, you can, boss, but others…"

"What you're saying there is troublesome, my little Météor."

"Why, boss?"

"Because I intend to send you to interview King Boris."

"Boss, I'll run all the way there," Météor exclaimed at once.

"What about those traps, those dungeons?"

"Oh! Boss, I'm not thinking about those any more, since it's a question of completing a mission that you've entrusted to me. And then, I've studied at your school! However, if there was to be any breakage, it would be much better if it was me who was toasted rather than you. I'm all alone in the world, and it would certainly be a much less severe loss for humanity than if you came to break your pipe."

"Do you imagine, by any chance, that I would want you to break yours?"

And seriously this time, the king of detectives said, "I rely a lot on you, not only because you do me greater service every day, but because you've shown me a devotion and a friendship such that I've attached myself to you with bonds of an almost paternal affection."

"Oh! Boss, boss, how happy I am to hear you talk to me like this! If I dared, I'd kiss you, but I'd better wait until New Year's Day, that will be more appropriate."

Chantecoq replied with a smile, "I'm glad to hear it and, even if there were some traps in the private home of this dreadful fellow who calls himself Count d'Esseck, I know you to be too skilled to fear even for a moment that you might fall into one.

"This then is what I want. You perhaps don't speak English and German very well, although you've made, I observe, great progress in both languages, since I asked you to study them.

"In any case, you're naturally gifted at imitating accents, which will easily allow you to pass in the sovereign's eyes for a native of one of those two countries."

"I think," declared Météor, "that I'd succeed best as an Englishman, so much more so as it's easier to do the disguise."

"Then let's go for the English," the great bloodhound decided. "I'm going, soon, to give you an identity card to which I'll attach a letter of recommendation from the English ambassador, which is, as it happens, authentic and served me well once in the course of an expedition where British interests were at stake."

"It's just a case of changing the date and the name, and all will be done.

"I'll have committed a forgery, of course, but since it's done with a good motive, I assure you it will inspire no remorse in me and it won't weigh on my conscience."

"I understand," said the secretary, nodding in approval.

The private detective continued. "Thanks to those two items, it will be relatively simple for you to get close to Boris, who has every interest in managing at the moment, not only the leaders of the great European powers, but also public opinion in those different countries. Ask him what he thinks about peace, about war, about commerce, about industry, about the arts, about cinema, etc. I know you're gifted with a rather fertile imagination, along with the most persuasive patter.

"In the end, when you've finished your little story and the king has responded in a more or less satisfactory fashion which, however, is not in any way important, ask him to be so good as to give you his most recent photograph for your journal."

"And if he refuses?"

"Then look out, you'll be sinking in my esteem, because you won't have managed to fool him. I'm convinced that by applying yourself, you'll get a result which is vital to me, as you'll see subsequently, if we want to find that poor girl."

"I believe, boss," replied Météor, "that you're in the process of engineering another of your formidable schemes."

"It's certainly possible," said Chantecoq. "I won't pretend, indeed, that this adventure doesn't inspire a little passion in me, and that's for two reasons: the first is that this idyll, shattered in such a tragic, lamentable fashion, has moved me deeply; the second is that I wouldn't be sorry to teach a harsh lesson to this truly ignoble king who believes he can act with impunity.

"If I'm talking to you like this, it's not only because I'm a republican, but above all, and I'd say even uniquely, because I consider that the higher placed miscreants are, the more severely they must be punished."

"Boss," concluded Météor, "I agree with you there."

Then he added, "What time do you want me to go and visit Monsieur Boris?"

Chantecoq reflected for a moment, then replied, "As soon as you're in disguise, you come back here and I'll give you the papers, which I'll have had time to adapt to your personality."

"Understood, boss! I too am happy, like you, to come to the aid of brave people. It's like in père Dumas: it's about, in life, conducting yourself like a musketeer, that's to say like people who do good for the sake of justice and who defend honour for honour's sake.

"And then, above all, still like in père Dumas, vice must be punished and virtue rewarded!"

"Go, my lad," invited Chantecoq, giving his secretary a friendly wave.

He pivoted on his heel and, in two steps and a jump, light as a squirrel, he reached a small door.

Chantecoq barely had time to see him open it.

Météor had evaporated.

Then the king of detectives gave a broad smile, and murmured, "This time I think I've found an adversary with whom it's going to be necessary to wrestle to the ground.

"But no matter, if victory is at the end of the fight. I believe in victory."

6 THE INTERVIEW

That same evening, around seven o'clock, a young man, elegantly dressed, with a very English style, who could have passed for an heir, a sporting champion, or a fashionable journalist, rang at the gate of King Boris's private home.

At once, he gave his card to the porter, who came to open the door.

Doubtless he was expected, because the concierge, after reading the card, led the visitor directly to the steps to the ground floor of the royal residence.

One of the panels of a large door, defended by an array of ironwork which was as artistic as it was solid, opened, revealing the silhouette of a footman dressed in a French uniform.

The porter announced simply, "Monsieur Richard Folkestone, the Paris correspondent for the great English newspaper, *The Times*."

The lackey must also have received some very precise instructions because, without answering the porter, he bowed respectfully before the new arrival and, in a tone full of ceremonious politeness, he asked him to follow.

Météor was in position.

The lackey showed him into a waiting room, decorated and furnished in ultra-modern style.

Some paintings hung on the wall, if one may grant that name to these pictures, which were as calamitous as they were flabbergasting.

Chantecoq's secretary cast an alarmed eye over these deformations, which were supposed to represent nude women.

"What a display of butchery!" he said. "Ah! I don't know what's wrong with artists today. They choose the most repulsive models; and thereupon, they flank you with the red and black and white and yellow and opulent green, as much as they can, so although the women look like cuts of veal, calves look like cuts of women and that puts you off it for life.

"It appears to be catching on. Recently I heard from my boss that one of his friends, a doctor, amused himself by collecting a full museum of this genre and that he paid twenty-five to thirty francs for most of the canvasses.

"But, one fine day, snobbery got involved; it was enough for five or six pundits to affirm that they were masterpieces. Then our doctor, born cunning, hastened to send his entire collection to the auction house; he earned a big chunk there.

"I'm delighted for him, because he's an amazing bloke, who spends his time helping people and he's one of those rare doctors in whom, these days, you can trust."

Météor had got that far in his medical aesthetic reflections, when the lackey reappeared, announcing, "If Monsieur would follow me. Monseigneur the Count d'Esseck will receive him now."

Climbing the staircase to the first floor, Météor thought, "What a guy my boss is! That didn't take long. In three hours, he succeeded in obtaining, thanks to the advice he gave me, an audience with this king who, it appears, is rather difficult to approach when not indulging in pranks."

As he reached the landing, he added to himself, "Now, watch out, my old Météor, try to hold up in the presence of this 'Count Five-Secs'."

The valet led him into an anteroom, where the two policemen Arad and Mako, disguised as old courtly fellows, seemed to be waiting to be received but, in reality, were mounting a vigilant guard over their sovereign.

"That's odd," Météor thought, "why am I going in before these two old duffers? I know a journalist can get in anywhere; but that doesn't mean anything. My flair, as my boss puts it, warns me that those two birds, more or less plucked, are in no way diplomats, or politicians on the lookout for a backhander."

The lackey opened a double door and announced in a formal tone, "Monsieur Richard Folkestone."

Météor went into the lounge at once, where we saw the tragic scene between Boris and Francine Gardannes unfold.

The king sat in an armchair, near a little round table on which a cigar case was half-open. Discreet lighting, coming from the ceiling, allowed the visitor to make out his features.

The king's face, while affecting superficial benevolence, wasn't without a hint of suspicion.

Boris's guard was up.

Météor bowed respectfully to him.

The king, who hadn't stood up, contented himself with responding with a small nod of his head and, after having launched a puff of smoke from his Havana towards the ceiling, he said, in a cold and distant voice, "Monsieur, what did you want with me?"

Météor, who wasn't the sort of man to feel intimidated,

even in the presence of a crowned head, replied at once, with an English accent that was so well-imitated that we can't reproduce it.

"Sire, I wanted first to thank you for the honour you do me, by deigning to grant an audience."

The King of Sokovia replied, "I'm not only a great friend to your country, but also a loyal reader of your newspaper. Not only because of the praise with which it's so often showered me but moreover, and especially because it is admirably informed and most pleasant to read."

Météor, affecting a keen satisfaction, said, "Would Your Majesty grant me permission to reproduce his declarations at the head of my article?"

"But of course, gladly," the amorous ogre accepted. "However, I insist, before it's published, that you send it to me, because I'm suspicious of these improvised conversations; however great your good faith may be, it could well happen that you, as certain of your colleagues have done, misrepresent the scope of my words and alter their meaning, to the point of making me say the opposite to that which I wanted to express."

"Sire, I bow to your will and, first thing tomorrow morning, I'll send Your Majesty my article typed up on paper with very wide margins. Your Majesty will be able to personally correct anything which doesn't please him."

Relaxing a little, Boris I said, "I see you're a very proper gentleman. I trust your word."

And, inspired by his usual slyness, he added, "However, and this is purely indicative, if, for one reason or another, you fell short of the formal engagement you just took with relation to me, and if your article appears in *The Times* without my approval, I would see myself absolutely forced to issue a denial."

"Sire," replied Météor, on top form, "you won't have that trouble. As I've already had the honour of telling Your Majesty, first thing tomorrow morning, my paper will be in your august hands."

"Then," the king decided, completely reassured, "interrogate me and I shall answer you."

Météor, who had prepared a whole series of questions that were carefully lodged in his memory, began resolutely.

"Sire, would I be indiscreet in asking what Your Majesty thinks of the global political situation?"

While pouting a little, the sovereign answered, "Oh! Monsieur journalist, you're not going to pull any punches and that first question you're asking me is both so important and so complex that I would need several hours to give you an answer.

"However, I must warn you that you're not speaking to Boris I, King of Sokovia. I'm staying in Paris incognito, under the name of the Count d'Esseck, and I believe I'd be lacking in the duty that French hospitality demands of me if, while in territory that is not my own, I sounded off on international politics with ideas that might not be entirely to the taste of France's leaders and the French people."

Not discouraged, Météor, who was a resourceful lad, replied. "I can only bow to your decision which shows how far Your Majesty pushes delicacy. So, I'll content myself with addressing the Count d'Esseck and asking what he thinks of the arts, of our modern artistic movement?"

The king didn't respond. This question seemed to embarrass him even more than the first. There was nothing astonishing about that, because he was devoid of all aesthetic comprehension and, on this subject, he deferred exclusively to his counsellor Rupert de Rurick, who barely had any more taste than him.

Seeing he was needled, Météor continued. "Just now, I was shown into a lounge whose admirable furnishing and decoration led me to think Your Majesty was somewhat taken with modern art."

Boris let out a grunt, from which it was impossible to judge whether he meant "yes" or "no". Imperturbable, Chantecoq's secretary continued.

"This magnificent room, in which I have the honour to find myself right now, can only confirm my opinion. I would therefore be curious to know which painters are particularly favoured by Your Majesty. Matisse, Modigliani, Vlaminck, Favory, Derain?[12]"

With an authoritative gesture, Boris I interrupted, saying, "I prefer Detaille[13] because of all the painters I've known, he knows best how to paint a uniform and a horse. As to those of whom you're talking, they might have a great deal of talent, but I wouldn't know anything about that. Anyway, I don't know of them, and I don't intend to get to know them. I abhor painting. If art is placed around me, it's because the walls must be garnished and one can't always use military trophies, the heads of stags or wild boar, or porcelain plates."

Météor thought, "What a brute!"

But Boris was off, Météor allowed him to unfurl his eloquence, and Francine's attacker continued.

"For me, painting is nothing next to cinema. Ah! Talk to me about cinema. That's art, especially the newsreels, when

---

[12] Artists mostly associated with cubism and fauvism. Bernède spelled at least two of their names incorrectly. Possibly this is a deliberate mistake, an indication that Meteor's not quite as polished as he's trying to appear, but I corrected them for this translation because that seemed like a bit of a stretch.

[13] Édouard Detaille (1848-1912). A military artist and "official painter" of battles during the Franco-Prussian War. Noted for his precision and realism.

we see a procession of emperors, kings, presidents, ministers, the army, magistrates, clergy, civil servants, etc; at least all that is alive, it's not fixed to the canvas, it exists, it works, it moves, it's slices of humanity."

"Bravo! Bravo! Sire," Météor said, all the time taking stenographic notes in his reporter's notebook.

The king, delighted at making a favourable impression on his interviewer, added, "For me, cinema's principal attraction is to draw my attention to very beautiful women that I would otherwise certainly never have known, if the Lumière brothers hadn't invented their machine. So, when one of them pleases me… let's stop there, because that would exceed the scope of an interview and I wouldn't want to say certain things that might be misinterpreted."

"Understood, sire…"

But Boris continued. "It's my turn, monsieur reporter, to ask you a question. As you're undoubtedly aware, I've been filmed quite often."

"I'll permit myself to add," Chantecoq's secretary insinuated himself, "that Your Majesty is extremely photogenic."

"It's been said in the past, and I've come to believe so," declared Boris with an expression of puerile self-satisfaction.

Then he said, "But there's one thing that perhaps you can explain to me. How is it that, even when you're filming in very fine weather, it's always raining on the screen?"

"Sire, it's not rain that you're seeing, it's wear on the film which produces rays, which produce, especially after a certain amount of time, the effect of a real shower."

"How curious," said the king.

Météor, who felt the time hadn't yet come to ask his host for a photograph, continued. "Might I now ask Your Majesty what his favourite films are?"

Boris answered, "I wouldn't like to upset anyone, or to offend any foreign sensibilities. However, in order to be loyal, I must declare that, despite the real masterpieces that certain American, German, Italian and even English studios have made, it's French films that I prefer.

"And you know why? Because of the Parisian women I meet. I always adored Parisian women. They're no better than others, sometimes they're far worse, but they have a peculiar charm to which I'm attracted irresistibly."

"Jackanapes!" thought Météor, noting all Boris's words with care. More and more lyrical now, the king was continuing.

"Nothing, indeed, surpasses a Parisian woman. I've heard tell that one of Turkey's last sultans filled his seraglio with them. How I understand him! And, if I was allowed to have a seraglio, I'd do just the same!"

Boris bit his lip and, understanding that he'd gone a little too far, he said, "You can cut that last sentence, can't you?"

"Your Majesty can relax completely," replied Météor.

And then he added, "No doubt Your Majesty has had a cinema installed in his palace?"

"I've had two installed," replied Boris, "one in which I gather my whole court every week, and the other, much more intimate, where I invite only the initiated. But cross out that sentence, too…"

And rejoicing at this game himself, the Count d'Esseck cried out, "There's nothing like an English journalist to get one talking about certain things."

Météor felt he'd earned the right to smile and the king, growing more familiar, said, "Take a cigar."

Chantecoq's secretary took one of the Havanas spread out in one of the case's compartments. He trimmed the tip with the help of a special cutter which was on the table, and lit it with the lighter that sat next to it.

The king pressed a buzzer and the lackey appeared. Météor, believing the audience was at an end, was preparing to formulate the demand which was the sole purpose of his visit, when Boris barked a few words in Sokovian at his lackey; then, he waved to Météor to stay.

Météor thought, "What's going on? He doesn't seem bright enough to guess who I am, so it's not a trap. So, as I appear to have impressed on him, perhaps he'll invite me to dinner. Now, that would be a true mark of success. That would raise me further in the boss's esteem and, after all, it wouldn't go down too badly if I could say nonchalantly to my friends, 'Oh yes, the other evening I had dinner with the Count d'Esseck.'"

This time, the brave boy's predictions were somewhat exaggerated.

Instead, the lackey returned with a platter which carried a flask filled with port and two very fine crystal glasses.

He placed it all on the table, near the cigar case, filled the two glasses ceremoniously, and withdrew with solemnity.

The king declared, "It's an old port that my cousin the King of Spain gave me as a gift. I believe it's the very last bottle in the world. Try some, Monsieur reporter…"

But, still cautious, Météor thought, "After all, you never know what might happen. Perhaps I was spotted by the two warders who were in the waiting room earlier. Perhaps Doris I here wants to spike me. Wait for him to drink first, that's the best bet."

He raised the glass in order to contemplate its contents. It looked like liquid rubies.

"What colour!" he rhapsodised.

Still playing for time, he sniffed it, saying, "What a bouquet!"

The king was still not drinking.

"Well then!" he said to Météor, "What are you waiting for, to sample this marvel?"

Artfully, Chantecoq's secretary replied, "Sire, I wouldn't permit myself to wet my lips in this glass before Your Majesty led the way."

Boris said with a smile, "In my whole life, I've rarely met an English reporter who knew court protocol as well as you."

And grabbing his glass, he swallowed several mouthfuls from it.

Météor said to himself, "Now I can go ahead without fear and that's no problem for me, because I think I'm going to regale myself with it."

The port, indeed, was a true nectar.

Météor felt he ought to exclaim, "Sire, this beverage is worthy of you, since it's worthy of the gods themselves!"

Boris adored flattery, as do all sovereigns, who consider their lot in life to be nothing but receiving universal adulation.

Completely won over by the fake journalist's crafty attitude, he said, "Do you have any further questions for me?"

Seeing he was so well-disposed, Météor thought, "This is the moment to risk the photograph request."

And he said, "Sire, I really wouldn't want to abuse Your Majesty's benevolence. Thanks to everything Your Majesty has deigned to tell me, I possess the elements for an extremely interesting article and I hope tomorrow, on reviewing it, Your Majesty will be satisfied with it."

"I'm sure," declared Boris, duped by his guest's manoeuvre, and he added, "I'm happy to demonstrate my satisfaction. If you have any favour to ask, I'd consider it a pleasure to grant it."

"Sire, would I be abusing your generosity if I asked you, for my paper, of course, to entrust to me your most recent photograph, so I may use it to illustrate my article?"

Boris who, deep down, had the soul of an old ham, could only feel highly flattered at this request, which seemed only too natural on behalf of he whom he had mistaken for the representative of one of England's greatest newspapers, and he replied at once.

"I can satisfy that request immediately."

And, taking a photo of himself, which was placed on a table of a most capricious and tormented design, he personally removed it from its frame and handed it to Météor.

He, affecting a respectful joy, replied, "Would it be too much to further abuse Your Majesty's benevolence if I asked him to be so good as to write his signature beneath this fine portrait, including the date of this day that I'll never forget."

As the monarch seemed to hesitate, Météor, who had been raised in a good school and had more than one trick up his sleeve, continued smoothly. "It's to give this royal photo a stamp of absolute authenticity."

Boris, who certainly seemed to have been won over completely by Chantecoq's secretary, took a pen from his jacket pocket and inscribed at the bottom of the photo:

To Sir Folkestone, editor of The Times.
Boris I, King of Sokovia.

And he added, "While we wait for the ink to dry, how about another glass of port?"

"Sire, you're spoiling me," replied Météor, while the Count d'Esseck, without taking the trouble of disturbing a lackey, filled the two glasses himself.

Météor said to himself, "I think this time, I've won at flirting. I can see the boss's jubilation from here when I bring him this document, thanks to which, I'm sure he'll be able to pull off some new and startling feat."

The king raised his glass and said simply, "To England!"

Although he wasn't in the habit of visiting kings, Météor was blessed with an instinctive tact, which prevented him from making a gaffe of protocol, as he touched his glass to His Majesty's.

"To Sokovia! To the king that it chose! To the noble Boris I! Father to all his subjects."

The amorous ogre gave a smile and muttered in a sly way, "Father to all his subjects, let's not exaggerate! Let's just say there are a few who owe their lives to me, that's entirely possible, but, after all, I know nothing about it and I'll wait for them to resemble me before I acknowledge it!"

Météor, understanding he would certainly have the opportunity to meet once more with Boris, said, in order to keep in his good graces, "Your Majesty is the world's most spiritual sovereign."

But as their throats were sufficiently dampened, the ink ought to be dry. Boris took the photo and handed it to Météor.

As a man who knew how to take care of his own publicity, he said simply, "On the front page, is it?"

Météor, who didn't feel constrained by any promise, since he found it impossible to keep any of them, replied with marvellous composure, "The front page, sire, at the top of the first column."

"That's perfect. Don't forget to bring your article tomorrow, at around nine o'clock."

"Sire, I have it in mind to prove to you that if punctuality is the courtesy of kings, then it must also be that of journalists."

Boris was so delighted with this interview that he held out a hand to his visitor. Météor shook it briefly with all the deference owed to sovereigns, and he left, backing from the room, saluting on several occasions he whom he had just played with such skill.

Jumping into a taxi, he hastened to return to Avenue de Verzy to rejoin his boss, who was waiting for him, while reading the stenography of the conversation he'd had with Robert Santenois and which he had arranged to be typed up by a second secretary, named Paul Landry, whom he had engaged some time previously on the recommendation of his son-in-law Jacques Bellegarde, head of news on the *Petit Parisien*.

When he saw Météor rush into his office, not having had time to remove his disguise, simply from the shining eyes that he turned towards him, Chantecoq understood his skillful collaborator had won a first victory.

In two bounds, Météor reached Chantecoq's desk and, without speaking a word, handed him the dedicated photo that he had received from Boris's own hands.

"Now that's some good work," said the king of detectives, approvingly.

He didn't need to say any more for Météor's face to take on an expression of intense jubilation and for him to puff out his cheeks fit to make them burst, which was for him the sign of the most complete jubilation.

Chantecoq, after examining the photo of the King of Sokovia with care, said, "There's one of the easiest heads to copy that I've ever encountered in my life."

"Indeed," declared Météor, "I noticed at once that he resembled you, boss! Oh! Only physically."

And coldly, the great bloodhound said, "I don't pretend

to be virtue personified, but, in any case, I'm not one to amuse himself by abducting an honest young girl."

"Oh, no, never," insisted the secretary with energy.

"Or to murder and chop her into pieces," intoned the famous policeman, with a slight tremor in his voice!

"Murder… chop into pieces!" Météor exclaimed, "What are you saying, boss, that's scary stuff, and you don't look like you're joking."

"Indeed, I'm not joking at all."

"What did you manage to find out?"

A telephone suddenly rang. Chantecoq took the device and listened.

"I can tell you nothing for the moment," the private detective soon said, "if only superficially…"

But he stopped, only to say a moment later, "There's someone else on the line, who's definitely listening to us. Are you far from here?"

"No."

"Good! Jump in a taxi and come and meet me here."

He hung up the receiver, then, addressing Météor, he said, "Go quickly and remove your make-up, and sit at your usual listening post, with your notebook and pencil in hand. I think you're going to have an important conversation to transcribe."

"What's going to happen, then?"

"I don't know yet: everything depends on the turn taken by the meeting I'm going to have with the person who called just now, that's to say, Monsieur Robert Santenois.

"It's highly likely that I'll need you in the course of this meeting. Then, give up your place to Landry and, in that fashion, we'll see what he's capable of doing."

"He seems to me to be very intelligent, filled with

goodwill, and I believe, boss, that he'll soon be of very real service to you."

"He's still a bit shy."

"That's understandable, isn't it? But don't worry, he'll come out of his shell, and fast…"

"Go then, go, holy chatterbox!" Chantecoq cried. "Santenois is going to arrive and you won't be ready."

The king of detectives hadn't even finished this sentence, but Météor had already vanished.

Chantecoq pressed a buzzer placed on his desk.

Almost at once, through the small door through which Météor seemed to have evaporated, a young man appeared, with distinguished features, clear, intelligent eyes, and who gave the impression of being a lad from a family which was both loving, and had raised him well.

"My dear Landry," said Chantecoq, "I'm expecting an important visit; but first I have a few questions: it was you, wasn't it, who typed up the conversation Météor took down in shorthand?"

"Precisely, monsieur, that was me."

"I must compliment you on it. Your work was carried out very well. You understood that the house motto is *fast and thorough*, I'm highly satisfied."

The young man nodded slightly. His apparent reserve contrasted oddly with his colleague's exuberance.

"Now, my dear Landry," continued the great bloodhound, "let's speak briefly, but to the point. I don't need to ask if typing up that conversation interested you because if it hadn't, you really wouldn't be right for the vocation of detective work. I've already observed, instead, that you're blessed with all the still embryonic qualities that this profession necessitates."

Paul Landry declared, "I must tell you, Monsieur

Chantecoq, that this case interests me greatly and I'll even add that it's moved me deeply."

Chantecoq retorted, "I greatly appreciate the first part of your response, and I was expecting it. As to the second, it pleases me much less and I'll tell you why at once.

"Although I'm not one of those who proclaims the human heart's weakness, I consider that a good detective must beware his generous impulses, especially when carrying out his work. An emotion, however legitimate, all too often loses, indeed, three quarters of your means.

"In police work, one must work only with one's brain and not with one's personal preferences. One must always proceed, according to the fashion in which the case presents itself, whether by deductive or inductive reasoning, and then, without looking backwards too much, think ahead, guided by a combination of instinct, understanding, reasoning, logic, flair… That said, I'd like you to express to me your strictly analytical impressions on the case that concerns us."

"Monsieur Chantecoq," replied Landry, "I've not had time to reflect seriously and furthermore, my inexperience leads me to fear saying things you may find puerile, even ridiculous."

"Speak anyway and above all with me, my dear, avoid all timidity. Proceed firmly and summarise in a few precise words, the reflections which crossed your mind."

"Monsieur Chantecoq," replied Landry, encouraged, "in my humble opinion, this abduction can only have been carried out by someone who has powerful resources at their disposal and who occupies a lofty position."

"What leads you to think that?"

"Certain details struck me. First, the dispatch of this fake clinic director who, to play such a difficult role or rather, to inhabit such a character, which must not have been his first, must be blessed with special aptitudes which, generally, are rather costly to remunerate."

Chantecoq gave an approving nod of his head.

Landry, further encouraged by his boss's attitude, continued.

"Furthermore, managing to keep Monsieur Robert Santenois in Rouen reveals a clever plan, necessitating a relatively large number of participants who would be amply compensated.

"I conclude that it's in the world of high society that the culprit must be sought, and I was particularly struck by the answer Monsieur Santenois gave you, when you asked if he might have had any significant encounters, with his fiancée, in the preceding days.

"Monsieur Santenois responded that he had, indeed, the opportunity to make the acquaintance of a certain Count d'Esseck. Now, this Count is none other than Boris I, King of Sokovia, the most degraded of beings, and capable of the most cowardly infamies."

"Therefore," asked Chantecoq, "you think he was behind the kidnapping?"

Landry replied with firm deference, "Indeed, monsieur."

And he added, "You're going to think, monsieur, that I'm perhaps a little daring, even reckless…"

"Not at all," Chantecoq assured him. "I'm rather delighted with everything you said, it proves you're blessed with a strength of reasoning and perspicacity seen only rarely in beginners. I'm glad to see it, because, in addition to the sympathy you inspired in me as soon as I got to know you, you're building my confidence in you, and that's enormous, for a beginner, to make his boss appreciate him like that.

"I believe I'll be able to entrust some interesting missions to you on this present case. Which will lighten the load a bit for Météor and myself."

There was a knock at the door: it was a valet who, beneath his livery, had retained a somewhat military bearing. At once he announced to Chantecoq, "It's Monsieur Robert Santenois."

"Good," said Chantecoq, "ask him to wait a few moments. I'm going to receive him…"

The servant took a few steps on principle and returned to the hallway. Chantecoq then said to his second secretary, "You join Météor, who must already be at his listening post. It's possible I may need him in the meeting I'm about to have with Mademoiselle Gardannes's fiancé.

"In that case, he'll pass you his pen and his notebook and you continue to take down our conversation. There, everything's going well and I have a feeling - what am I saying? - I'm certain we're going to have a lot of fun. See you soon, my friend."

Paul Landry went out, leaving the detective alone. He pressed his buzzer. The valet reappeared and, opening the study door, he made way for Santenois, who entered the room.

7 THE MACABRE DISCOVERY

The young engineer appeared even more overwhelmed than the first time he had entered the detective's office.

Pale, distraught, his eyes haggard, he held an unfolded evening newspaper. And, at once, he stepped towards Chantecoq, saying, "It's horrible… it's her… I'm sure of it… it's her!"

"What's the matter, Monsieur Santenois?" asked Chantecoq.

"You've not read the article in the *Intransigeant*?"

"Which article?"

"The one which talks about the discovery in scrub ground close to Saint-Ouen, of a young woman's arm, which was wearing on one finger of her right hand a ring bearing the initials *F.G.*"

"Yes, I read it," replied Chantecoq.

"And you didn't think, you, the greatest of our modern detectives, that this arm and this ring might belong to my fiancée?"

"For a moment," declared Chantecoq, "I had that notion,

125

but I thought about it. And I told myself that, however capable of anything King Boris might be, I doubt however that he would have gone so far as to murder your fiancée and dispose of her in such a dreadful manner."

Santenois objected. "He won't have acted himself, he'll have entrusted the job of carrying out his crime to the bandits with whom he must have surrounded himself."

"Ah well! My dear monsieur," replied the king of detectives, "I'm not of that opinion at all, and I'm going to tell you why.

"For all that my flair - and I wasn't mistaken - warned me it was indeed Boris who kidnapped Mademoiselle Gardannes, that same flair warns me this unfortunate young girl is still alive and that it's not her arm that's been found, but that of another."

"And the ring?" asked Robert, breathless.

"The ring…" repeated the great bloodhound. "Nothing would have been easier for Boris than to get hold of that."

"To what end?"

"Well, let's see, to put it on the finger of that human debris which his agents, to whom you just alluded, procured for him. And all so as to let it be thought that Mademoiselle Gardannes had been drawn into an ambush, murdered, and chopped into pieces.

"But rest easy, no other parts of her body will be found. In any case, this is what I propose to you, so as to reassure you completely and to make you share my opinion.

"First, one word… have you noticed any distinctive features on the arm and hand of Mademoiselle Gardannes?"

"She had a beauty spot on her right forearm, and on her left elbow."

"Then all is well. If you don't feel brave enough to

confront the sight of this macabre discovery, do you want me to go to the Medical Institute alone?"

"No, I'd prefer to accompany you," replied the young engineer. "You've instilled such courage and comfort in me that I'm again ready to hope."

"There's a first success, for which I congratulate myself," Chantecoq concluded.

He pressed the electric buzzer.

Météor appeared instantly and Chantecoq said to him, "We're leaving, Monsieur Santenois and myself, to run an errand. Meanwhile, prepare outfits number 21, 24, and 37. You'll put on 24, and give 37 to your colleague Paul Landry. I'm reserving 21 for myself."

"I suppose, boss that it's about to kick off," declared Météor, who seemed delighted at the mysterious decision that his boss had just taken.

"Go, hurry, my absence will be of very short duration."

Météor melted into the air.

As to Chantecoq, he left his study with Santenois, took his overcoat, his hat from the hallway, left his home, crossed the Allée de Verzy and hailed a taxi, which brought him directly to the Medical-Legal Institute.

Chantecoq sent his card to the director, who received him at once.

The detective and the civil servant knew each other well, and if the second had a deep respect for the first, it nourished a deep admiration for the ace of aces among detectives.

In a few words Chantecoq explained the purpose of his visit to the director.

The director replied that, indeed, the sinister debris had just been brought to him and that he had not yet placed it in the refrigeration device.

With complete discretion, without even asking Chantecoq the reasons behind his enquiry, he said, "If you want to see it at once, I'm completely at your disposal."

Chantecoq accepted and, following the civil servant, he went with Robert Santenois into a laboratory.

The arm in question lay on a marble slab.

Robert stifled a cry, having noticed on the amputated arm's elbow the beauty spot he had described to Chantecoq.

The director looked at him, astonished, worried. But the great bloodhound hastened to declare, "Monsieur is the fiancé of the young girl to whom he believes this arm may have belonged."

"Ah! Monsieur," said the director, "I understand your emotion. It's such a dreadful thing. I may have been made blasé about this kind of thing, but it's always painful to witness the despair of a man in love. But perhaps you were mistaken. It's only a coincidence."

Santenonis replied, choking back his tears, "She was also wearing a ring with her initials *F.G.* which I gave her. That's it, I can see it there on her finger."

"Then, there's no doubt, monsieur. It's dreadful, abominable!"

Meanwhile, Chantecoq was carefully examining the distinctive sign that the supposed young girl's arm bore.

He didn't spend a single moment looking at the ring.

Robert continued to weep hopelessly, when Chantecoq straightened up and said in a firm, decisive voice, "Monsieur, cease your despair. I give you my word this arm isn't Francine's.

"The proof is that the beauty spot, which convinced you so painfully, is purely artificial. It's been made, skillfully however, with silver nitrate. You don't need to be a chemist to be sure of that."

The director of the Medico-Legal Institute took his turn to lean over the human debris, examined it carefully with a loupe, then declared to Robert, "Monsieur Chantecoq is absolutely right, see for yourself, monsieur."

Robert dared to approach and he cried out, "Yes, it's not her arm, it's not her hand, her fingers were much more slender, more tapered."

"So you see," Chantecoq cried out in triumph and, clapping the young engineer's shoulder affectionately, he added, "Now do you trust me, Monsieur Santenois?"

Francine's fiancé declared, reassured, "I beg your pardon, Monsieur Chantecoq, for ever having doubted you, but I was beside myself. Now, it's finished: I'd follow you to the end of the earth."

The king of detectives replied, "I won't ask you to make quite such a long voyage with me, but it may be that I'm soon called upon to ask you to accompany me on a rather lengthy trip."

"I'll do so gladly," replied the young man.

"And you'll be right," said the director of the Medico-Legal Institute. "You have the good fortune, monsieur, to have our national Chantecoq as a guide, and with him one never encounters error or defeat."

"Monsieur director, I beg you," said that great bloodhound, smiling, "you'll make me blush like a peony. In any case, thank you for your kind welcome, which allowed me to reassure Monsieur Santenois and proved to me once more that, whatever some of my young rivals may say, I still have a little flair."

"More than all of them put together," cried the civil servant.

The three men exchanged handshakes and left the Institute.

As they were about to get back in a taxi, Santenois said to Chantecoq, "I'm going to ask you another great service."

"Tell me, I beg you."

"Before returning to your home, if you could accompany me to Madame Gardannes to reassure her, just as you've reassured me. She'll believe you more easily than me, because she'll imagine, if I tell her that her daughter's alive, that I'm trying to take care of her and prepare her gently for the dreadful news. That's why…"

"Say no more," interrupted Chantecoq. "Your request is so noble that I'll hasten to carry it out."

"You're kindness itself, Monsieur Chantecoq."

"Oh! I'm not always so obliging, especially when carrying out my job."

"I can't believe that," insisted the young engineer, who gave the driver Madame Gardannes's address.

When they arrived on Rue Saint-Vincent, Robert's first act was to ask the chambermaid who had come to open the door, if she hadn't received the news!

"Oh! Monsieur, don't ask me about that," replied Mariette. "Earlier I bought a copy of the *Intransigeant* which was being sold in the street."

And with her eyes full of tears, she added, "That poor lady… it's dreadful!"

"Don't worry," said Santenois at once, "it's not her. I've great hope that Mademoiselle Francine is still alive."

"Oh! Monsieur," cried the brave girl, "if you could only imagine how happy I am to hear you say that! Mademoiselle is so good, so gentle and she's beloved by everyone."

Santenois replied in an anxious tone, "Madame Gardannes hasn't read that newspaper?"

"Monsieur, I've done everything to ensure that no one

other than I has entered her bedroom. It's a blessing that Madame can't move at the moment because, if she read what was written in the *Intran*, she would surely have dropped dead on the spot."

"Please tell her," said the young engineer, "that I wish to see her with a person who's accompanying me, and that I have some interesting news about Mademoiselle Francine."

Immediately, Mariette vanished, only to return a few moments later to announce, "Madame will see you now, Monsieur Robert, along with this other gentleman."

After leading them down a corridor, she showed them into the poor mother's bedroom. Lying in an armchair, she represented the very image of suffering.

"Yes, my dear child?" she said, holding out a trembling hand to Robert.

It was all she could say; her dry throat prevented her from speaking, and her eyes were spilling tears abundantly.

"Madame, I'll begin by telling you that although, for a few hours, I've lived through some dreadful moments, I'm now reassured as to the fate of our poor Francine."

"Really!" Madame Gardannes exclaimed. "Oh! Tell me quickly…"

While pointing out the great bloodhound to her, Santenois continued. "Thanks to Monsieur Chantecoq whom I have the honour of introducing to you and whose name and reputation you certainly know, I'm certain, not only that Francine is alive, but that we ought to find her soon."

A ray of hope illuminated Madame Gardannes's despairing face, and she replied in a less anguished voice, "Monsieur Chantecoq, it's really you, the famous detective? Monsieur, I know your name already. Your son-in-law, Monsieur Bellegarde, who publishes such interesting articles in the *Petit Parisien*, is a close friend of one of my relatives,

Monsieur Delaurier. I've met him several times at my cousin's home, along with your daughter, they were very kind to me."

Chantecoq gave a deferential bow to Madame Gardannes, who continued. "Monsieur, I bless the heavens at the thought that you'll busy yourself finding my darling child: because, as Robert just said, you'll find her, I'm sure of it; and my gratitude, believe me, will be boundless."

"Madame," replied the detective, "I'll do everything to procure that happy ending. So far, nothing leads me to fear failure. What I can tell you, but I beg you not to ask me anything further…"

"Rest assured, Monsieur Chantecoq, I'll behave myself."

"Then," replied the bloodhound, "all I can tell you is that, first, your daughter is alive. Second, I know her abductor. Third, I'm certain he may be attempting to isolate her, but at all costs, he doesn't want to draw attention to her existence.

"It may be, however, so as to allay suspicions, distract public opinion, and frustrate my investigations, that he may spread rumours, with so-called proof attached, that Mademoiselle Francine has been murdered.

"Don't believe a word of it! I swear to you, on the life of my daughter, who is everything I hold dear in life, much as your daughter is to you! Madame, I'll finish by begging you, instantly, so as to be able to move quickly and avoid any sticks in the spokes, which would be a simple indiscretion to me, not to make a report to the police.

"Given the kidnapper's status, which I don't yet feel able to discuss, the intervention of the Quai des Orfèvres[14] would serve only to complicate things and delay the moment where you can finally embrace your dear child.

---

[14] French Scotland Yard.

"I'll also ask, if you see any strange people, even close friends, to maintain an attitude which leads them to think you despair of ever seeing your daughter again!"

"That will be easy," replied Madame Gardannes, "I've already felt such sorrow at being separated from her, and to think she's exposed to such danger and she's in the hands of people capable of anything. It will be easy to convince visitors that, in my sorrow, I've hardly any hope."

"Well, madame!" Chantecoq replied, "Quite the reverse, you may have a great deal of hope… just don't show it, that's all. Now, permit me to take leave of you, because, from this evening, I'm going to not launch myself into the campaign, because that's already done, but to mobilise, because I'm in a hurry to see a happy smile succeed your tears."

"Once more, monsieur, I thank you," said Madame Gardannes.

She held the detective's hand, who squeezed it respectfully. Addressing Robert, Chantecoq said, "I need you tomorrow at nine o'clock. Stay and keep Madame Gardannes company."

"Oh! Yes, Robert, stay," asked the poor woman, "we can talk about her."

Chantecoq added, "And await her return in all safety."

8 THE FESTIVAL OF THE LITTLE WHITE BEDS

Chantecoq returned home directly. He found his two secretaries there in costume, one as a Maharajah, and the other as a Harlequin.

They were both so well disguised, that at first glance the great bloodhound hesitated to pin a name on the two individuals.

But one having lowered his mask, he recognised him to be Paul Landry and, at once, he said, "My dear, you just committed a small error, or rather, I ought to say, a big one. Your clothes are perfect, you wear them boldly and with a great deal of elegance; you look absolutely like an actor from the old Italian comedy. But remember this principle: it's not enough to wear a mask over the face in order to be completely unrecognisable.

"That mask can slip, it can be torn from you, and then, you're recognised... burned. So, while I'm putting on a carnivalesque costume myself, ask your kind friend Météor to arrange a head which will render you completely unrecognisable."

And he added, "Let's all three of us go into the laboratory."

It was a huge room which rather gave the impression of the pharmacies in which modern doctors pursue, with varying tenacity and luck, studies aiming to scrutinise nature's secrets.

One whole side was taken up by an immense cupboard with sliding doors which contained the complete collection of Chantecoq's disguises.

"First," said the detective, "what time is it?"

"Half past six," declared Météor, consulting the watch hooked to his wide, clinking, Maharajah's belt.

"It's too early for dinner," declared Chantecoq. "However, as we must have an excellent supper this evening, there's no point in filling our stomachs too much, especially as during the course of the evening we'll need all our physical agility and cerebral activity.

"So, my little Météor, take this acoustic horn, blow it with every ounce of puff in your lungs, and warn our brave cook Marie-Jeanne that she should send, through the intermediary of her husband, a half dozen good sandwiches, accompanied by two carafes of beer.

"In this fashion, we won't have heavy stomachs and this evening we'll be able to not only taste a menu such as I've rarely enjoyed in my life, but give free rein, before pleasure, to all the fantasies that circumstances may demand of us."

It was easy to see, from the expression on the faces of the two secretaries, that they were wondering what new surprise their boss had in store for them.

They didn't doubt for a moment that they would have to go to a large costumed ball.

But where? With what aim?

It was clear it wasn't just to dance, or to eat. There was another reason. What? The Boris case, probably. Both of them, well aware of the great bloodhound's habits, were careful not to pose him the slightest question, and Météor immediately obeyed his master's injunction. Chantecoq began to carefully examine the clown's costume, which lay over a chair, glittered with spangles.

With a smile, he said, "This is going to rejuvenate me somewhat! Indeed, the first time I disguised myself in this, it was to catch a fairground owner who had murdered his wife. I was still a Sûreté Générale agent. I was just getting started in my career, young and full of ardour.

"Well! My God, I notice one thing, after all, even if this costume has been very well preserved and not deteriorated, I still feel, thanks to the careful and brief physical exercises I run through every morning, whenever I have time, I feel almost as supple as then and even capable of jumping through a hoop, if necessary. I hope we won't be forced to go that far."

While he was indulging in these reflections which revealed, on his part, a youthful character and optimism so well designed for facilitating his task, Météor had enveloped Paul Laundry in a large sheet and sat him on a chair, in front of a table furnished with a mirror and flanked by two powerful electric lamps. Then he set to work drawing and painting a black mask on his face, of the exact dimensions of the wolf he had adapted for himself previously.

"You see, this way," he said, "if your mask slips or is stolen, you'll still be masked. It's very important."

Soon the valet Pierre Gautrais, a former soldier who had served under Chantecoq during the Great War and once saved his life, appeared, carrying on a dish the ordered sandwiches, as well as two carafes of beer, to which he had added three glasses.

He put everything on a table and with that deferential familiarity with which he was accustomed to address his former commanding officer, he said, "Marie-Jeanne is kicking up a hell of a fuss."

"Why?" asked Chantecoq.

"Because she made, for this evening, a chicken with mushrooms which was already smelling so good it made you want to taste it before it had even finished cooking…"

"Oh well! My friend, you'll both enjoy it," replied Chantecoq.

"It will be far too much for us."

"Come, come," joked the king of detectives, "don't be coy with me, you'll get through it all. You're both of a size, Marie-Jeanne and yourself, to cope. If your wife can stand up to a cock, I'm sure you're incapable of resisting a chicken for long."

"Oh! Monsieur, what a dreadful opinion you have of me!"

"It's not a reproach I'm making, far from it! Now, go back to your better half and tell her that, for the next few days, I'm rather afraid she won't have a great deal of cooking to do for me."

"So you're getting ready to leave for the field?" Gautrais retorted.

"I can't hide anything from you," said Chantecoq with a smile.

And, patting his shoulder, he said, "It may be that, soon, I'll give you the order to mobilise."

"Boss, I ask nothing more," cried Gautrais, "when it comes to adventures it's some time now since you dropped me, you know I'm never so happy as when fighting the good fight with you."

With that, he left.

"What a brave lad!" Chantecoq said, when he'd gone.

"And his wife!" Météor interjected. "Boss, you're lucky to have two such servants: he's as devoted to you as a guard dog with teeth that could chew through rocks, and the other's a cordon bleu who could feed an archbishop. I'm sure you'd need a long time to find a better one."

"Meanwhile," said Chantecoq, "let's do justice to Marie-Jeanne's sandwiches."

They disappeared quickly, as well as the two carafes of beer. Then Chantecoq, removing his civilian clothes, picked up a sheet in turn, sat at the table and, with speed and an extraordinarily steady hand, made himself a clown's face, which had one incontestable superiority over that of Fratellini: a natural gaiety, which could only communicate itself to all those it met along its way.[15]

Let's add that as well as wearing make-up, he was absolutely unrecognisable.

Then he put on the spangly costume, similar to that once worn by the famous Foottit[16], the Nouveau-Cirque's genial clown whom no one yet replaced and whom doubtless no one will ever replace.

He topped himself off with a little white felt hat and, his costume complete, after having indulged in a few rather successful capering leaps, and some no less remarkable perilous standing jumps, he began to walk on his hands with such agility that Météor cried out, "Sweet! There's some footprints on the ceiling."

---

[15] The Fratellini family were a circus family who became extremely popular in France after the First World War, and well into the 1920s.

[16] George Foottit (1864-1921). An English clown who found huge fame and popularity in France.

Paul Landry, who had never yet seen Chantecoq carry out such a sensational number, said, "Monsieur Chantecoq, permit me to offer you my sincere compliments. I know plenty of acrobats who wouldn't be capable of that."

Chantecoq, who had resumed the natural position nature has given to man, replied, "I'm not displeased and I think that, this evening, we're going to have some fun. Now, my children, listen to me. I need, before we leave, to give you some explanations and also some advice."

We shan't reproduce the conversation that Chantecoq had with his two secretaries, not because it was devoid of interest, far from it, but because we prefer to take the public straight to the events which follow and not to deprive them, through premature explanations, of the surprise I felt myself when Chantecoq first gave me his account of this adventure.

As a result, my dear readers, I beg you to follow me, in thought naturally, to our national theatre at Opéra. Not to witness any ordinary performance, sometimes very ordinary, of *Faust*, *Roméo*, *Hérodiade*, or *Lohengrin*, over which the dust, accumulated in that vast edifice which is so difficult to sweep, has fallen and falls every day, like a black snow under which those masterpieces of the repertoire are destined to disappear. No, we're going to witness a great party held by an evening newspaper, the *Intransigeant*, a party called "the little white beds".

Let's say, in parentheses, that this is an admirable work, which has the aim and result of improving the fate of childhood and does the greatest honour to its founder, Monsieur Léon Bailby[17], director of the newspaper that we

---

[17] Léon Bailby (1867-1954). A highly influential French press baron. The sports supplement for the *Intransigeant* is a dim ancestor of *Paris Match*. The ball of the little white beds was real, and was launched in 1921. It was essentially a benefit evening for children with tuberculosis.

just named, as well as to his colleagues, and notably to Madame Henri Lavedan, the eminent academic's wife, who consecrated to this foundation all the treasures of her generous activity and of her benevolent heart.

Around ten o'clock in the evening, the party began to become hugely animated.

On a silver bridge, placed above the hall, all the Parisian celebrities wanted to come and parade before the public who were welcoming them with enthusiasm.

In a booth, three masked people were witnessing this spectacle, truly worthy of the Opéra theatre; there was a clown, a Harlequin, and a Maharajah, in other words Chantecoq, Paul Landry, and Météor.

Soon, Chantecoq leaned close to the ear of this last and said, "Go and check he's arrived."

Météor slipped from the booth, went down a corridor, and entered the hall.

Mixing among the numerous groups which crowded around, he managed with skill to place himself in such a way that he could recognise and count the people occupying the boxes.

Doubtless he had fulfilled the object of his mission because, almost at once he went to rejoin his boss, and said to him, "He's there."

"Alone?" asked the king of detectives.

"No, with three old blokes, who look to me rather more like policemen than diplomats or chamberlains."

"No women?"

"Not one woman!"

"You're sure you're not mistaken?"

"You can rest easy on that, boss. I had him in my eye… that's our weirdo."

"Then he's not disguised?"

"No, he's just got a domino mask, like his companions."

"Good, thank you. Now, you can listen to Mistinguett at your leisure… she's extraordinary!"

And, leaning towards Landry, he whispered a few words to him, after which he stood up and left the booth in his turn.

But, instead of going into the hall, he went into the public foyer, transformed into a refreshment room full of small tables and, approaching one of the waiters, he asked him, "I should like to speak to the butler looking after the reserved seats."

The waiter pointed out a man in a suit who, very officiously, was going from right to left, stimulating the zeal of the legion who were finishing up the five hundred covers for the nocturnal feasts.

Landry, truly an incomparable Harlequin, approached and asked him, "This afternoon, you must have had a telephone call from the Foreign Secretary reserving a table with three covers?"

The butler took out a notebook which he consulted. "Indeed, monsieur."

"As the Minister requested, that table is right next to the Count d'Esseck's?"

"Yes, monsieur."

And the butler, puffing himself up suddenly, asked, "Will we have the honour of serving the Minister?"

"No," replied Paul Landry. "For a long time, Monsieur Briand[18], whenever he can, has the good habit of going to

---

[18] Aristide Pierre Henri Briand (1862-1932). A French statesman, who served *eleven* terms as Prime Minister during the Third Republic. He was also Prime Minister between July and October of 1929, the year this book was published. A key figure in post-War

bed early and, this very evening, he's retired to his property in Cocherel…"

"Where there are also some chicks," emphasised the butler, who was trying to be witty.

"Yes, but not the same kind."

The butler gave a little sneer: he had understood.

Then he said, in a satisfied tone, "Thank you, monsieur, for warning me that the Minister won't be occupying that table in person; because you're getting me out of an embarrassing situation."

"How so?"

"I'll tell you frankly: the beautiful Kadina…"

"The Moulin Rouge dancer?"

"Yes. She asked me to place her as close as possible to her sovereign, to whom she wants, she told me, under the cover of a mask, to give a big surprise. So could I use the table? I can give you another a little further away, but I guarantee you'll be very well placed."

Paul Landry replied, "I greatly regret being unable to do you this service, but the table has not been retained for the Foreign Secretary in person, but for three special agents from Quai d'Orsay, of whom I'm one, with the mission of watching over His Majesty's safety."

"Is an attack feared?"

"Perhaps," Chantecoq's second secretary dared to affirm, "but let's keep that between ourselves. I'm speaking to you because, first, when I have such an important mission, I have a principle of seeing it through, and also because I intend to preserve your own responsibility."

Disoriented, the butler said, "Monsieur, you can count on

---

reconciliation in Europe, in 1929 he tried to establish a "European Union" which was scuppered by the rise of Fascism in Europe..

me completely. It's very serious, it's even excessively serious, and it's certain, if an attack were to happen, that would be dreadful."

And he added, in a tone of comic fright, "So long as Boris isn't going to ruin my night!"

Anxious to get in the good books of this secret agent, who represented for him a force so much more considerable as it was occult, the butler said, "Would you like me to show you to your table at once? That way, you'll have no trouble finding it."

"Gladly," said Landry.

The butler, leading him to the other end of the foyer, said, "You can call me Désiré, that's my baptised name. All the snobs in Paris know me and call me Dédé. It seems I resemble Chevalier[19]. Is that true?"

Paul Landry who, for his part, judged it was in his interests to get along with the butler, replied, without hesitation, "Oh yes, you do look like Chevalier! I could almost believe you're his brother."

Désiré, delighted, replied, "I sing and dance as well."

"So, gifted as you are, why not embark on a career in music-hall?"

"My wife doesn't want me to."

"She's jealous?"

"Like a tigress. Perhaps she's right, because, with a physique such as mine, it wouldn't take long for me to be harrassed. I'm already very sought after."

"That doesn't surprise me. But, you love your wife?"

---

[19] Dédé is a three act opérette first performed in Paris in 1921, which helped launch the career of Maurice Chevalier (1888-1972). Yes, the actor who sang *Thank Heaven For Little Girls* that closes the film *Gigi* (1958). A song title that's not aged well, but he also sang the title song for Disney's *The Aristocats* (1970).

"Not at all; but she's Paul Lormier's niece."

"Paul Lormier?"

"The famous bookmaker."

"Does he give you tips?"

"No. I wouldn't want him to: I'm no gambler, but he's leaving his entire fortune to my wife in his will. As she stands to gain ten million, you'll understand I'm not inclined to divorce her."

"I understand you. Completely." Paul Landry declared.

Désiré replied, pointing out a rather well-placed table, near one of the windows which looked out over the loggia, "That's where you'll be…"

"Perfect! And the Count d'Esseck?"

"There, you see, you'll be nearby so you'll be poised to fly to his aid if anyone suspicious gets too close."

"Then it's all perfect, Monsieur Désiré. I'll make the Minister aware of how obliging you've been with regard to our task, and I'm sure he won't forget you."

"If only he could send me a dozen eggs from his chickens," said Désiré. "That would do me a greater service than any other."

"Why?"

"Because then I could invite Uncle Lormier to lunch, prepare for him a splendid truffle omelette and say, 'This omelette was made with eggs which came from Monsieur Briand's chicken coop.' I'm sure after that he would take me to be a great man."

"You'll get your dozen eggs," replied Landry, "I'll undertake it as a personal duty."

Radiant, the butler accompanied the Harlequin up to the foyer doorway and, after having given him the most zealous salutations, he turned back to his staff, who he began to chew out with a facility for elocution that could have made him a remarkable parliamentarian.

Landry got back to Chantecoq's booth, and reported on his mission. The king of detectives appeared very happy and, doubtless reassured for the rest of the evening, he let himself be taken away by the pleasure of the show, shining above all, which was unfolding before his eyes.

Soon, he stood up and, flanked by his two acolytes, he roamed the hall, the corridors, climbed up to the boxes and, when it was time for supper, he was one of the first to enter the foyer.

Guided by Landry, he reached his table and sat down, while talking in a low voice to Météor, who found himself placed nearby, "I think we're going to have some fun."

The vast hall, brightly lit, sumptuously decorated, was soon filled with an elegant crowd in multicoloured costumes, with ladies rattling with pearls, diamonds, weighed down by magnificent jewels. It was a true fairy tale spectacle, worthy of our great Paris of luxury and art.

One table remained unoccupied: that of King Boris.

"By Jove!" Chantecoq thought, "What if, at the last moment, through one of his caprices, he abandoned his plan to dine here, to go and slum it in some Montmartre or Montparnasse dive?"

He was going to send Météor on reconnaissance, when Boris appeared, flanked by the three old men serving as his entourage.

As we've already said, deep down, Boris had the soul of an old ham.

While living incognito in Paris, not only was he horrified at passing unnoticed everywhere he went, but he intended, above all, that it was known the Count d'Esseck was actually the King of Sokovia, and it rather displeased him not to be recognised at once when people passed him.

His intimate advisor, Rupert de Rurick, had, on several occasions, observed that this attitude wasn't entirely prudent, but he replied, "I've nothing to fear, when Arad and Mako are with me! And I laugh in the face of assassins.

"My people consider me to be a mannequin, which doesn't bother me, and as a result I have no revolution to fear, no attack! Let's live joyfully, therefore, and not in fear!"

That evening, Boris had done everything to draw the crowd's attention to himself. It was so much easier for him as he was well known to all the people who thronged into the Opéra, and he had the satisfaction of hearing murmurs all around him.

"Boris is here... Boris is here!"

Which, according to him, would consecrate him in what he called his Parisianism.

In an ostentatious fashion, distributing smiles to the men and winks to the ladies, he reached his table, at which he sat with his three bodyguards.

Placed as he was, Chantecoq missed none of the four characters' gestures and actions.

He didn't intend to listen to their conversation, because he strongly suspected they would be speaking in their national language, which he didn't know and which he had never fancied learning. He was not mistaken.

Boris and his retinue who, however, were only conducting a faintly animated conversation, were expressing themselves in Sokovian throughout the meal.

Towards the end, Boris, who alone had drunk his way through two bottles of champagne, began to suppress a few yawns.

His Majesty was visibly bored and he was finding this supper, however charming, not sufficiently in line with his personal tastes.

Ah! How much, indeed, to this meeting of the Parisian elite, assembled with the aim of easing the suffering of the smallest, would he prefer those nightclubs of which nine tenths are owned by foreigners, and for which other countries reproach us so severely and so unfairly.

But the king, although incognito, was a person who was too much on display to give the signal to depart himself.

He was therefore waiting for a few carousers to desert their tables in order to let out a sigh of relief and ask his special advisor, still in Sokovian, "Where shall we finish the night?"

Paul Landry, who had his back to the king and had, throughout the meal, lent an attentive ear, hoping in vain that he would pick up an interesting word, heard the counsellor list the names of various nocturnal establishments which flourish in Montmartre.

He noticed, no less distinctly, the amorous ogre respond in French this time.

"No, not Montmartre, or Montparnasse. I hear there's a new Russian club, which is rather curious. They've called it, I believe, *Douma*."

One of the three assistants clarified. "I know it, we can go there safely, it's well frequented."

"Then I'm not going there," Boris refused. "This evening I've seen some overly distinguished people; and as I love a contrast, I'd like to go to a place where there's some real scum."

Rupert, irritated, objected. "Sire, I beg you, give up this scheme, your face is so popular that you might be recognised, and if there are no revolutionaries in that happy nation called Sokovia, there are in France a certain cosmopolitan underworld which pledges mortal hatred to all sovereigns and heads of state, and wouldn't be upset at the opportunity to take one out."

"Oh well! I'll think about it," decided the amorous ogre, particularly attached to his own skin.

While he was smoking a fat cigar and his three companions were exchanging anxious glances, Paul Landry leaned over to Chantecoq and quietly repeated the words he had just overheard.

Chantecoq tilted his head, which meant, "thank you"; then, without even taking time to reflect, he called a waiter, and asked him to fetch a pencil and a blank sheet of paper. The waiter brought over the requested objects at once.

With one object, Chantecoq scribbled a few lines on the other, refolded the paper and, passing it to Paul Landry, said to him in a low voice, "Slip this message to the old fart behind you, and try, above all, to avoid the king seeing your movement."

Landry gave a nod of acknowledgement and, very carefully, did as Chantecoq asked.

The counsellor was at first a little surprised at the contact of this paper which was brushing his hand; but, suspecting that it might be something important, he was careful not to let his surprise show on his face and, keeping the paper, he managed to place it on the table behind his plate; he unfolded it slowly, and without having attracted Boris's attention, he read the following:

Your three neighbours at the adjoining table: the clown, the Harlequin, and the Maharajah, are none other than three secret agents, charged by the government with watching over the Count d'Esseck's safety.

If the Count d'Esseck wishes to end his evening elsewhere, let us join your party, to better protect his person;

we've had wind that a conspiracy which is non-political, but organised by some simple individuals, seriously threatens your master's life.

We stand ready to join our efforts to your own.

Meanwhile, receive our distinguished salutations,

Brinquet, Lafargue, and Falguar.

PS: If you accept our proposal, you only have to turn your head and scratch your nose, while looking at the clown.

Rupert appeared highly intrigued by this message, and he glanced swiftly to the other two guests who, as our readers have guessed, were none other than Arad and Mako; then, under the table, he slipped the note to Arad and, to distract the king, began talking to him with a certain volubility, which allowed Arad to peruse the missive, which he passed to Mako.

When he too had finished reading, the three gazes of the counsellor and the two minions met in an expression which suggested they were of a mind to accept the offer which had been made to them, and Rupert, turning back towards the neighbouring table's occupants, scratched his nose, so indicating to the clown, that's to say Chantecoq, that he was in agreement.

Then he turned back to Boris, who still seemed plunged in a dreary ennui, and said in French, loud enough for his neighbours to hear.

"I think I've got it. They just opened, in the area of Avenue du Bois du Boulogne, on Rue de la Faisanderie, a new jazz club, extremely curious; it seems you can meet all sorts of people, and, since Your Majesty wishes to slum it, I believe you will find the opportunity to do so there."

"So be it, let's go to this club. What's it called?"

"Zoo-Dancing."

"Zoo-Dancing?" repeated Boris, who hadn't completely grasped the meaning of this term, which came from both Greek and from English at once.

The counsellor explained, "It means 'dancing-animals'."

Boris added, with a smile, "Just as a zoological garden means a park with exotic beasts?"

"Quite so," agreed Rupert.

"Very well! Let's go to the Zoo," said the king.

Mako left at once to fetch Boris's car.

The counsellor darted a swift glance towards the three private detectives that he had just mistaken for official detectives.

Chantecoq, who seemed to be delighted with the success of his ruse, said to himself, "I believe we're not going to waste our time, and that tonight, we're going to learn quite a few things."

9 AT ZOO-DANCING

His Majesty Boris I's counsellor was certainly marvellously well-informed on all our capital's inglorious spots.

The Zoo had been open only for a few days, and it had succeeded up to that point, despite a cacophonous advertisement, in attracting only a clientele that was hardly commendable. Yet God knows the organisers of this jazz hall had made every possible effort to satisfy the bizarre, often stupid and sometimes ignoble tastes of our contemporary snobs.

The hall was vast, spacious, surrounded by cages furnished with very narrow fences, which opened and closed at will; the centre was occupied by a remarkable floor, on which the dancers' feet could slip only with the most agile of steps.

Clever, varied lighting, shimmering in successive colours, produced strange and suggestive effects on all those who were jiggling on the dance floor.

The management had taken care to recruit its staff among the most beautiful people of colour who, deserting their original countries, had come to bring to Paris the sombre note of their persons, and the gay note of their frolics.

Some women, doubtful at first, mixed among them, forming a sort of human cluster of beans pressed close, which seemed to throb to the beats of riotously exasperated jazz.

On leaving the Opéra, Chantecoq had time to murmur in Rupert's ear, "We're following you, rest easy. There's a bar at your dance hall?"

"Yes."

"Well then! We'll install ourselves there, and you come and find us, because I have to talk to you about some very interesting and even very serious things."

The counsellor said simply, "Understood."

Half an hour later, at the Zoo, Boris had a cage opened, and he entered loudly, as was his habit.

The clown, the Harlequin, and the Maharajah, sat at the bar on large stools, and ordered a bottle of champagne.

They had been there barely five minutes when a man in a suit, with greying hair, and a pointed beard of the same shade, approached them, without appearing to notice them in particular.

Chantecoq and his two secretaries recognised him as one of the three people escorting Boris.

He sat on a stool next to Chantecoq, ordered a cocktail, then, when he had taken a few sips, he leaned towards the king of detectives and said, "It was you, wasn't it, monsieur, who managed to get a note to Counsellor Rurick which I then read?"

"Indeed, it was I," replied the great bloodhound.

"So, you're Monsieur Brinquet?"

And pointing out the Harlequin, Chantecoq made the introductions, "Here's Monsieur Lafargue."

Then, presenting the Maharajah, "And here's Monsieur

Falguar."

"And I," replied the bearded man, "I'm Monsieur Arad, the Count d'Esseck's chief of police."

"Delighted, dear monsieur."

"Likewise."

Arad explained. "Counsellor Rurick apologises for not having come himself, but he considered this business was more in my domain, that's why I've come to ask for a few explanations."

"Dear monsieur," declared Chantecoq completely amiably, "I'm quite ready to give you the necessary information, but I have a duty to request the most absolute secrecy."

"You can rest assured on that account," affirmed the Sokovian policeman, "you have my word."

"Even to say nothing to the king?"

"Why?"

"Because it's pointless to alarm him, especially as I'm even now working to frustrate the intrigues which seek to envelop him and which could very well end up in assassination."

"Damn!"

Chantecoq fixed him with his most penetrating gaze, and said, "Until now, there's been no danger in this building, but it's high time to inform you."

"What's all this about?" Arad asked, whose curiosity was making him over-excited.

"I'll tell you, but not here, because we must avoid indiscreet ears, and they could be all around. I saw, just now, a few unoccupied cages in the hall. I'll take one, and all four of us will go and occupy it. There, we can talk at our leisure."

"Understood!" the Sokovian agreed.

Chantecoq was about to fetch his wallet from one of his clown costume's inside pockets, but Arad beat him to it. Taking a thousand franc note, he gave it to the barman, saying, "I'll get this."

The king of detectives tried to protest, but didn't have time. Arad said to him in an extremely friendly tone, "Given the service that you're in the process of offering my master, it's only natural that I buy you some champagne."

He took the change that the barman brought him on a small dish. Without taking the time to slip the notes into his wallet, he stuffed them in his trouser pocket and, with an urgent air, he led Chantecoq to the waiter who rushed, thanks to the two hundred franc notes that Arad gave him, to open up one of the most comfortable cages for them.

All four of them entered, sat down, and Chantecoq, after having closed the door and raised the bars which led to the floor, began.

"Monsieur Arad, I'm now going to tell you the truth at once: Madame the Duchess de Castrovillari recently made the king sign a will, thanks to which she'll receive, on the death of your sovereign, a sum of ten million, plus a very fine castle in Sokovia, plus two million in jewels, of which a certain number belong to the Crown."

"You are marvellously well informed, Monsieur Brinquet," acknowledged Arad who, despite his professional skill, was a hundred miles from sniffing out, beneath the fake secret agent, the formidable king of private detectives.

And he continued, "His Majesty, indeed, has signed that pledge, or rather that legacy, and that was in spite of the respectful observations made to him by the President, which he didn't take into account at all. Now, Monsieur Brinquet, please continue."

Chantecoq replied, "Madame the Duchess de

Castrovillari, who, it seems, has never felt any sort of love towards King Boris, or any friendship…"

"That's still the case," confirmed Arad.

"I was saying, then," continued the great bloodhound, "that the duchess, anxious to obtain as soon as possible ownership of the means that your king is leaving to her, has decided to get rid of him as quickly as she can and, naturally, very shortly indeed.

"Fearing the consequences of an act as dangerous as it was criminal, she had recourse to another woman whom she charged with attracting the king to her home and giving him a lethal injection which, it seems, leaves no traces of toxins in the victim.

"I don't know who this woman is; she is, I believe, of foreign origin. I wouldn't even be surprised if she was from your country. We've not yet been able to check. But we know her precise address and we can easily, if you see no objection, not only hand her over, but take you to her and there, we four, we can easily grill her and make her confess the truth. This result would have a double advantage: that of opening the king's eyes over the actions of his dreadful favourite and, greater still, of preventing him from being assassinated."

Finally falling into the very skillful trap that Chantecoq had set for him, Arad, who loathed the duchess and who knew her to be capable of anything, replied at once.

"Dear monsieur, I can't tell you how grateful I am for the precious information you've just given me. It goes without saying that I accept your proposal with the greatest eagerness.

"If you want us to arrange a meeting tomorrow, I'll make it a duty to report, in your company, to this person from whom, as you said, we'll end up extracting the most complete confession."

Chantecoq concluded. "Even if we're forced to use the most... energetic methods..."

"Precisely," the Sokovian agreed.

And he added, "I see, Monsieur Brinquet, that we are perfectly suited to get along together."

"I was already sure of that," replied the king of detectives, "and, if you like, as I've no intention of lingering in this dive which, far from amusing me, inspires profound disgust in me, I'll ask if you could tell me what time tomorrow I might pass by to pick you up, to take you to the destination."

Arad thought for a moment; then said, "To avoid all suspicion, would you care to meet tomorrow, around three o'clock, at the entrance to Monceau Park, which is on Boulevard de Courcelles?"

"Perfect."

"All right."

Arad asked, "I ought to, of course, disguise myself?"

"Indeed, because we will also be disguised ourselves. I'll be an old provincial notary."

"And I'll be a pearl seller... felt hat, yellow gaiters and a little suitcase in my hand. How will you introduce me to this young person?"

"As the owner of a foreign music hall, anxious to sign her up as a star?"

"She's an artiste, then?"

"A dancer, very beautiful, and not without a certain talent."

"Then it's agreed, Monsieur Brinquet," concluded the king's detective. "Tomorrow, three o'clock, Monceau Park."

He held out his hand to Chantecoq, who shook it with an effusion which seemed completely genuine. Arad did the same with Météor and with Landry, who adopted the same attitude as their leader, and the three Frenchmen hastened to get outside and jump swiftly into a taxi, which took them back to Avenue de Verzy.

On the way, Chantecoq maintained a silence which the two secretaries wouldn't even have dreamed of disturbing. It was only after several minutes that he decided to break it.

"Ah! Monsieur Arad, you may be sly, or rather a rogue stripped of all scruples, but I'll prove that a French detective, of cast-iron honesty, can put you in his pocket with a thumb and index finger."

Météor and Landry exchanged a joyful glance: from the moment that the boss was happy, they were happy too and, without even wondering what methods Chantecoq was going to employ in order to win his cause, they made, each of them, the same reflection.

"As the boss puts it: the case is in the bag."

***

Chantecoq returned home with his two secretaries. All three went into the laboratory to remove their costumes. When that was done, Météor, as the most senior, asked, "Boss, what are your orders for tomorrow?"

Chantecoq answered, "Everyone needs to get up at eight o'clock. First, breakfast. Then, while I'm working on my side of things with Landry, you, Météor, will take care of preparing outfit numbers 11, 19, and 24."

"Splendid, splendid!" cried Météor, puffing out his cheeks fit to make them burst.

"What's wrong with you?" asked Chantecoq.

"I've never seen such a thing…"

"What? What haven't you seen?"

"A memory as prodigious as yours! To think we've over four hundred costumes in our repertoire and yet you never get the numbers wrong. That, boss, is what they call having a super-noggin."

"Hold your tongue, you vile flatterer. And now, my children, good evening… good night… It's three o'clock in the morning and five hours of sleep for you, who are young, isn't too much, especially with the various exercises we're going to be forced to undergo tomorrow and doubtless also in the days to come."

They separated in order to go to their respective bedrooms.

Chantecoq lodged and fed his two secretaries and they never had cause to complain, as they were treated like the house's children.

According to his habit, Chantecoq went into his bathroom, ran himself a rather warm bath and plunged into the tub.

"Now," he said, "let's put a little order not to our ideas, but to the execution of our plan. Let's see what I have to do tomorrow, before noon.

"Procure a location… that's done! Get a dancer to come… I see! Warn Santenois and that poor Madame Gardannes they'll have to make their way to the place in question… that's not difficult.

"The locale, I have it, it's the pied-à-terre of my children. As to the dancer, I'm simply going to ask my daughter to play that role. Before she was married, she was my secretary for several years, and none better than she could fulfil the rather delicate role I'm reserving for her.

"As to Santenois, I can count on him. Madame Gardannes, we can arrange to take her out… I've got it! She

158

knows my son-in-law. I'll ask Jacques to fetch her in his car.

"And then I mustn't forget the chambermaid… in the end, all that seems to be going very well."

Getting out of his bath, after having given himself a serious rubdown with some eau de Cologne using a horsehair glove, he put on some pyjamas and went to bed.

Less than two minutes after lying down, he was sleeping like a baby.

Those who are already familiar with Chantecoq's adventures will doubtless remember that he possessed a double gift which was endlessly valuable to him: the ability to fall asleep at will and to wake himself in the same manner, without requiring the services of an alarm clock, which sometimes break down.

So the following morning, when the hands of his clock marked eight, he sat up in bed, fresh, rested, ready to resume the fight, or rather to get back to the chase.

He got up, carried out his ablutions, shaved carefully, dressed, and went down to the dining room where he met his two secretaries, who arrived together, proving that the movements of the house's inhabitants were regulated with mechanical and mathematical precision.

All three did justice to the vanilla chocolate and buttered toasts that Pierre Gautrais served.

Without having made the slightest allusion to the day's business, Chantecoq said to his two collaborators, "My children, we're going, if you would be so good, to return to our rooms to dress. Let's reconvene in one hour in my study, where I'll explain the day's programme to you."

It all happened just as he said.

At the appointed time, the king of detectives and his two secretaries were in conference and, as we've taken to doing, so as not to further anticipate the events which follow, we'll be careful not to lend an indiscreet ear to the words they exchanged, so much more so as we're immediately going to discover their results.

10 WHERE THE DETECTIVE CHANTECOQ GIVES A SOKOVIAN POLICEMAN THE BEST LESSON THAT HE'S EVER RECEIVED

At around three o'clock in the afternoon, Arad, who had put on the costume that he'd described to Chantecoq the previous night, took, as had been arranged, the hundred steps in front of the gates of Monceau Park, which are on Boulevard de Courcelles. He didn't have to wait long, because, hardly had he begun this stroll than a man, dressed in a tall hat, a black frock coat, his face framed with an almost white beard, and accompanied by two men, dressed very simply and with the timid and somewhat self-effacing appearance of young provincial apprentice clerks, approached him and said, "Everything's going marvellously."

Arad gave a start of surprise. The individual bore such little resemblance to the clown whose acquaintance he had made the night before, that, at first glance, he couldn't believe it was him.

Chantecoq whispered in his ear, "It's me, Brinquet."

"Ah! Very good," said the Sokovian policeman, "my compliments, you're completely unrecognisable."

"You too," the king of detectives assured him, "if you hadn't given your signal, I'd never have spotted you."

"Oh! Well, I," said Arad, "I have such a habit of dressing up that it's become child's play to me."

Chantecoq, laughing into his false beard, continued with complete seriousness, pointing out his two collaborators.

"There's the Harlequin and the Maharajah with whom we enjoyed champagne last night."

"Monsieur Lafargue and Monsieur Falguar," said Arad.

"Hush! Not so loud!" hissed the fake notary.

And approaching King Boris's damned minion, he said in a low voice, "This is how it's going to work. I'm going to go with my two clerks to visit the dancer and I'm going to tell her she's just come into an inheritance. After ten minutes, come up, hand your card to the chambermaid, asking her to take it to her mistress. Take care to slip a ten franc note into the hand of that young person. Mademoiselle Casilda, that's her name, will ask you to go into a neighbouring room. We'll leave rather rapidly to make way for you, but we'll stay in the hallway.

"So, you'll begin the conversation with Mademoiselle Casilda. You'll tell her you've come to offer her an engagement overseas, etc, etc…

"When you've primed her, I'll return with my two colleagues, and then you let me lead the dance. I guarantee, Monsieur Arad, the business will be swiftly taken care of. That's agreed, isn't it?"

"Agreed."

With that, Chantecoq hailed a passing taxi, he showed in Arad, then sat down next to him.

Météor and Paul Landry sat facing them, on the folding seats. Chantecoq gave the driver the address: 22 Boulevard de Clichy.

They arrived promptly, because that day, exceptionally, there wasn't much congestion on Place Moncey where generally one is forced to wait for five, ten, fifteen minutes, sometimes longer, before crossing the true chaos where the police themselves have so much trouble to navigate.

As he got out of the car, Chantecoq paid the driver and said to his companions, "I'm going up first... follow me."

Then, turning back to Arad, he said, "You can come and join us in six minutes. It's on the second floor, the door on the right."

Chantecoq, Météor and Landry entered the building, climbed the staircase, and stopped on the second floor.

The great detective rang at a double door, which opened just a crack, then opened wider, so as to let the visitors enter, and closed mysteriously behind them. Arad, who was throwing himself gladly into the subtle trap that Chantecoq was preparing for him, paced the pavement for a few moments, then consulted his watch.

Eleven minutes precisely had passed since he had left Chantecoq.

He decided to take his turn to climb the two floors and went to ring at the door.

A chambermaid opened the door and asked him, "Can I help you, monsieur?"

Arad replied, "I should like to see Mademoiselle Casilda, regarding a very important matter."

The maid answered him. "Mademoiselle is very busy at the moment with some legal gentlemen, but, if you would like to give her your card, I can take it through to her."

Conscientiously observing the instructions that the

pretend Brinquet had given him, Arad took his wallet, took out a card and a ten franc note and slipped both into the chambermaid's hand.

She said, "I'm going to see, I'll be back in a moment."

Barely two minutes went by before the maid reappeared, saying with a smile, "Mademoiselle will receive you. She asks you to have a little patience. It won't be long. If you'd like to come with me?"

"Certainly, mademoiselle," agreed the Sokovian policeman who was obliged to silently acknowledge that the French policeman was an ace.

He followed the chambermaid, who led him into a pleasantly furnished boudoir, separated from another room by a simple curtain.

That room certainly had to be the lounge, because voices were raised in turn and sometimes at the same time: those of the fake notary and of the mistress of the house.

From some words which reached the Sokovian's ears from time to time, as he knew French in its most delicate nuances, it was easy for him to realise that they were talking business and that this young choreographic artiste was more than happy to discuss her interests.

A quarter of an hour passed; then, Arad heard the fake notary's voice speak up and say, "So, mademoiselle, we're in agreement. You have only to pass by my office in Louviers where we'll be finished with the legal formalities for which your presence is required."

"Understood, monsieur," declared the young woman.

There was a noise of chairs being pushed back, footsteps, a door opened, closed again, and, a few seconds later, the chambermaid entered the boudoir, announcing, "Monsieur, Madame will receive you now."

She lifted the curtain and Arad saw, in the middle of a

164

highly intimate-looking lounge, a very pretty young woman, dressed in a simple but elegant housecoat, and who seemed much more like a reasonable woman of the world than a giddy dancer.

"Hold on," he said to himself, "I didn't imagine she'd look like that."

He took a step towards her, bowing deeply to her.

Very graciously, Mademoiselle Casilda pointed him to a seat on which he installed himself.

Then he began.

"Madame, I beg your pardon for addressing you without having been introduced by anyone formally, but having had the opportunity to watch you dance, I had only one desire: that of seeing you take part, as a star dancer, of a troupe that I'm in the process of recruiting for a very grand music-hall, which has just been constructed in Buenos Aires."

"Monsieur," replied the dancer, "I'm extremely flattered to have attracted your attention. I don't doubt your proposals will be extremely flattering. But allow me, before entering negotiations, to ask why you had the peculiar notion of coming here with a false moustache, a wig, and make-up which, though very skillfully executed, have nonetheless aroused my curiosity and suspicion?"

Arad shuddered and said to himself, "I'm burned!"

Completely disconcerted by this twist that he would never have expected in a million years, he replied, or rather he babbled. "But mademoiselle, you're mistaken! I assure you that…"

With a swift gesture, the young woman removed from the visitor the black moustache that he'd glued under his nose and the wig of the same shade with which he hid his baldness which was as premature as it was absolute.

Arad stood and, letting out a cry of rage, he shouted,

"There's an act for which you'll pay dearly."

But he didn't have time to carry out his threat.

A double door opened. Chantecoq, Météor, and Landry leapt on the Sokovian and immobilised him in less time than it would take to describe.

Then, pushing him backwards into an armchair, Chantecoq, drawing a Browning from his pocket, aimed it at Boris's damned minion, saying, "If you shout, if you move, you're dead!"

Arad didn't want to speak or to move, and still less to die. He therefore obeyed the injunction from the king of detectives. Straight after, through the door which had been left wide open, a woman appeared, riding in a small cart that was pushed by Robert Santenois.

That person was none other than Madame Gardannes, Francine's mother.

Behind them was the chambermaid Mariette.

Arad, who had seen them, understood everything and said to himself, "I've been truly rumbled! There's only one policeman in the world capable of inventing such a trap and making me fall into it, the famous Chantecoq. Oh! He's all we needed on our heels. Now, I fear, all is lost."

Chantecoq turned back to him, and, while keeping his revolver pointing at him, asked Madame Gardannes, "You see this man, well! Tell me if it's indeed he who came to you under the name of Monsieur Levitz, director of a clinic situated on the Boulevard Delessert?"

Madame Gardannes looked hard at the wretch, then, in an assured voice, she replied.

"That's him, all right!"

"And you, mademoiselle?" Chantecoq asked Mariette, who had approached.

"I also recognise him, yes," declared the chambermaid,

with no less energy.

Chantecoq, turning back to his prisoner, said to him, "I hope, now, that you're going to acknowledge in turn that it was indeed you who, under the orders of the Count d'Esseck, led Mademoiselle Gardannes into an ambush."

"I've nothing to say to you," retorted Arad.

"Take care!" threatened Chantecoq.

"Or what?" exclaimed the Sokovian. And, sneering, he continued. "I'm fine. Since you're convinced that I know of the young woman's disappearance, and I do, you won't kill me. You're too skilled for that, Monsieur Chantecoq."

"Hold on, you've recognised me then, since earlier?"

"Yes!"

"How so?"

"By your actions."

"Ah well! It's true, I am Chantecoq, and as Chantecoq has it in his head to drag the truth out of you, he will manage it. You'd therefore do much better, as we say in police slang, in France at least, to lay your cards on the table at once."

Arad riposted, "Do what you want with me, I'll never betray my king's secrets."

"That's already one point to me," said the king of detectives with his ironic smile.

"What's that?" exclaimed Arad.

"You just told me you'd never betray your king's secrets. Therefore, just as I thought, it was King Boris who kidnapped Mademoiselle Gardannes."

This time, the Sokovian fell silent. He understood that he was no match for such a formidable adversary.

Chantecoq continued, completely calm. "Monsieur Arad, although you've acted in the most disgusting fashion in this business, I don't consider you to be the principal author of this crime.

"You've done nothing but obey, and it was he who gave the orders who is the main culprit. But rest assured, I have no intention - no one here has any intention - of provoking any scandal. We want to recover Mademoiselle Francine and we will recover her.

"You understand that I wasn't fooled for a moment by the sinister joke you played, trying to convince justice and public opinion that Mademoiselle Gardannes had been murdered.

"That business of the severed arm, the ring, all that was nothing but misdirection. So Mademoiselle Gardannes is alive, you know where she is, and I'm asking you to tell me."

"I repeat, Monsieur Chantecoq, that I've sworn silence and I will be silent."

"Monsieur Arad," replied the crafty bloodhound, "you see this poor woman who stands before you and who, overcoming the pain from which she's suffering, wanted to be brought here so as to confound you. You can imagine the terrible pain which tortures her. It's enough to look at her, this unfortunate; her full martyrdom is painted over her face!

"Have pity on her, have pity too on this young man who stands by her side and who is the fiancé of that poor child, victim of this abominable abduction to which you lent such a cowardly hand.

"Examine your conscience, ask yourself if you have the right to torment these two hearts any longer and if, even at the cost of your job, you don't have a duty to ease their distress."

"And afterwards?" asked Boris's damned minion.

"Afterwards, monsieur, your conscience will be at peace."

"Quite possibly, but I'll lose my job."

"Why should you care? You're rich, I know that. It's not even a question of money, which ought to embarrass you. But you have lavish appetites: you wish to become even richer. You're therefore no more than the most contemptible and most odious…"

Arad remained silent.

In a trembling voice, Madame Gardannes cried out, "Monsieur, I beg you, give me back my daughter! Tell me, where is my child?"

"Yes, speak," insisted Robert, "he won't do you any harm, I swear to you…"

"And if I keep quiet?" the rogue blustered.

Chantecoq said, "I ask for a word, and I will have it."

And, bringing his face close to King Boris's accomplice, he thundered, "You're in my power, you're my prisoner, you're my hostage! There's no use resisting me, I won't let you go!

"I warn you then that if, within forty-eight hours, you've still not told me what's become of Mademoiselle Gardannes, I, your sole judge, obeying nothing but my own conscience and my ardent desire to punish a criminal, I condemn you to death, and I will be your hangman."

"So, you'll know nothing," retorted Arad, who had become pale.

"Your colleague from yesterday, citizen Mako, whom I'll also manage to draw into a trap, which he won't avoid any more than you did, will perhaps have an easier tongue to loosen."

Arad thought, "He, I'm sure of it, would talk. Better get myself out of harm's way at once."

"And if I tell you the truth," he said out loud, "what will become of me?"

"You'll be saved," replied the king of detectives with an accent of sincerity which would have convinced the most sceptical. "But you'll remain my prisoner until such time as we've received proof you've told the truth and we've recovered Mademoiselle Gardannes. Then, you'll be hanged or guillotined elsewhere."

Arad thought, "I'm caught. This Chantecoq will do everything he says, to the letter. And he's right, I'm rich. I can live in comfort, independent, happy. I'd be wrong indeed to sacrifice my life for Boris who, in the end, is just an oik."

And aloud he replied, "I'll talk."

Madame Gardannes gave a sigh of relaxation.

Chantecoq recommended to Arad, "Above all, no funny business, no lies, remember what I told you and bear in mind that I will be implacable."

Arad replied, "What I'm about to reveal is the whole truth. After I obeyed the king and brought him into Mademoiselle Gardannes's presence, she, to escape him, tried to throw herself through the window. She did in fact jump out of the window."

"My God!" said the mother, with a sob.

"Calm yourself, madame, she was only wounded very slightly in her fall. It's then that we brought her back into the house. At that moment, the king's lover, Countess Barbara de Castrovillari, arrived and tried to kill the young girl, who had fainted. And she poured two drops of potassium cyanide on her eyelids."

"That's dreadful!" exclaimed Madame Gardannes.

"Don't panic, madame," continued Arad, "since your daughter is alive. Having learned some time ago that the Duchess de Castrovillari went about with a flask of that violent poison in her bag and fearing she would use it against my master, I succeeded in pinching it and replacing it with a highly anodyne substance.

"I am perhaps a very bad man, but, believe me, I beg you, I would never consent to making myself accomplice to such a cowardly murder and the fact I preserved the life of that young person will earn me, if not your pardon, then perhaps a little indulgence.

"Then the prince, to whom I had communicated that Mademoiselle Gardannes was in no danger, first thought to make me take her to Sokovia. It was I who ought to be charged with that transfer, but he changed his mind, finding that escapade a little too hazardous for the moment.

"Mademoiselle Gardannes is still in the king's private home, in a secret room, where she is cared for by an excellent doctor."

"Then she's still ill?" Madame Gardannes asked.

"No, she's only in pain and aching from the fall that she had, and above all broken by the emotions she has endured. The king is waiting for her to be strong enough to travel to Sokovia, because he doesn't despair of overcoming the energetic resistance against which he has been rebuffed until now."

"Ah! I can finally breathe again," cried Madame Gardannes, shaking Robert by the hand.

Completely carried away with emotion, Robert declared, "Monsieur Chantecoq, I believe victory is at hand!"

"Yes, yes, quite so," said Chantecoq, "but the battle isn't over."

And addressing Arad, he said, "I told you I was obliged to keep you at my disposal, until such time as I could not only verify your statements but also to recover the young person that we're looking for. I haven't the slightest intention of throwing you into a dungeon, of tying you up, gagging you, or committing the slightest act of abuse towards you.

"I want only one thing: that's for you to keep quiet, not get involved in anything, and that the time which passes, you should pass it as agreeably as possible, that's to say by sleeping.

"As I'm not a hypnotist by trade, I'm simply going to give you a slight jab in your arm, which will cause you no pain and which will put you into a sleep that I'll renew, if it should prove necessary. I promise your life is in no danger, but you will find yourself much better for this forced rest to which I condemn you.

"You must have a bit of arterial tension, Monsieur Arad, well! This will lower that for you. Meanwhile, I'm going to take you to the bedroom which is set aside for you; you'll only have to lie down on the comfortable bed in there, give me your arm with full confidence and a few seconds later, you'll be asleep.

"It even appears that the substance with which I'm going to inject you procures dreams and visions which are much more pleasant than those induced by opium and other such substances. When you awake, I'm certain you'll say, 'Monsieur Chantecoq, you've been spoiling me'."

Arad thought, "He's certainly making fun of me, but what good would it do to resist him? Now I've told them everything; there's nothing to do but to submit to his will. Anyway, I believe he's too loyal to send me into the next world."

Preceded by the so-called dancer Casilda, who witnessed this whole scene, and flanked by Chantecoq and by Météor, he entered an adjoining room, a rather vast bedroom, and went to lie down, just as the king of detectives had ordered him, on a divan in the centre of the room.

"Please take off your jacket," Chantecoq invited him.

Arad obeyed. The detective continued, "Now roll up your

172

shirt sleeve."

Arad carried this out with the same complicity.

Then, taking a pouch from his pocket, which contained a Pravaz syringe[20], filled with a yellowish liquid, and an injection needle, which, very carefully, he sterilised in the flame of a candle, Chantecoq fixed the needle to the syringe and, with the skill of a professional, he gave the Sokovian's arm the jab he'd promised.

This injection, as he predicted, must have been absolutely painless, because King Boris's minion didn't even flinch. A few seconds later, his eyelids closed.

Chantecoq, turning towards the pseudo-dancer, said to her, "Now my dear Colette, I entrust him to you. You can relax: he won't give you much trouble watching over him. He's now going to sleep for at least forty-eight hours. Anyway, so you're completely at ease while your husband is out, I'll send you my old Pierre Gautrais. With him, you can relax: he knows the setpoint."

"Understood, father," replied Casilda, who was none other than Madame Bellegarde, daughter of the king of detectives.

Both of them, leaving behind the Sokovian policeman in the arms of Morpheus, god of sleep, went back to the lounge to rejoin Madame Gardannes and Robert Santenois.

Both seemed full of hope.

Madame Gardannes cried out, "Monsieur Chantecoq,

---

[20] Named after Charles Pravaz (1791-1853). Pravaz was a French surgeon who invented the hypodermic syringe, as a development of Irish doctor Francis Rynd's hollow needle in 1844. Pravaz's needle was made of silver, and the syringe was operated by turning a screw rather than pressing a plunger. Of course, if it was a genuine Pravaz syringe that Chantecoq's whipping out, then the barrel would be made of silver too, so we wouldn't be able to see the liquid inside. Glass-barrelled syringes were first developed in 1866.

once more, thank you, and you too, madame, who were good enough to play a role in this business where my entire life is at stake."

"But, madame," declared Colette Bellegarde, "it was only natural. First, how could I not oblige a father such as mine and then, how could I fail to be interested in the fate of a young girl who is such a great artist and who I only needed to meet two or three times for her to inspire my most sincere affection?"

"So," said Chantecoq, "everything's going terribly well. Now, it's a question of finding a trick to force His Majesty Boris to hand over Mademoiselle Francine. Ah! That trick, I think I have it."

11 WHERE KING BORIS HAS
A RATHER BAD DAY...

Arad had told the truth.

Mademoiselle Gardannes was indeed imprisoned in the Parisian home of Boris I.

Chantecoq, without having any material proof, was absolutely convinced of this, because he told himself quite rightly that Arad wouldn't have been in the mood to lie to him.

The problem that posed itself for him, was working out how he could obtain the unfortunate young girl's liberty from her abductor.

But Chantecoq wasn't the sort of man to hesitate for long.

Without being one of those foolhardy and reckless improvisers who, after having launched themselves on a risky route, falls at the first obstacle, he had nevertheless taken a prompt decision and, as soon as he had taken that decision, he carried it out with a speed that could be qualified as methodical, so much was it based as much on audacity as on cunning.

This is what he'd already said to himself:

"To find the hiding place where Boris has locked up Mademoiselle Gardannes, is to raise the alarm, and it's certainly possible that this abominable rogue wouldn't hesitate to remove the living witness to his infamy. There's no point addressing him directly, so let's employ a ruse."

Returned home, he went to his office, lit a good pipe and, after having walked for a while up and down his vast study, he sat at his desk and took out the photo of Boris. For almost an hour, sometimes using a loupe, he examined it with the greatest care, as though he wanted to impregnate his memory with this lofty personage's physiognomy.

Then he took his pen and tried to imitate the king's handwriting, taking inspiration from the dedication at the bottom of the portrait. That required at least two good hours of work, at the end of which he managed to imitate the amorous ogre's signature with such perfection that it was impossible to distinguish the forgery from the authentic one. He called in Météor and Landry.

"We're nearing our goal and I hope to be finished with it this evening. You can take this afternoon off. Use it to get some rest and, if needs be, to take a good siesta, because there's every chance that tonight will be as thick as one of Marie-Jeanne's onion soups.

"This evening, straight after dinner, take out costumes 22 and 39."

"That's it!" cried Météor, who knew the famous repertoire of disguises as well as his master did. "I'm going to dress up as a woman once again."

"It really suits you," retorted the great detective. "So long as, in any case, you're not trying to pass yourself off as an ingénue, you still produce your little effect. But now, I must ask you not to interrupt me any more with your reflections, sometimes funny, but rather often preposterous. You'll do me the honour of listening in silence.

"So, I'll continue. When you've dined, around half-past eight, both come to Prince Boris's house and tell the porter that you were summoned by him. You, Météor, you've already worked in the house, and you know your way around. However, I'll take care to provide you with a letter of introduction, which will open all the doors to you.

"Landry, you'll be the director of the International Bank of Europe and Asia, and Météor, you'll be the director of the *Gazette du Petit Sou.*"

Météor couldn't keep himself from exclaiming, "Sweet! I'm going to do my little 'Madame Hanau'. Let's hope it will get us into a private office other than that of the prosecutor."

"Now," said Chantecoq, "go and get some rest. Before leaving, I'll give you the document in question. I have time to fabricate it, it won't take long. I'll leave it on this table hidden under a fold and you'll just have to pick it up when you depart.

"Go, my dear friends, and see you soon! This afternoon and for a part of this evening I'm going to be adventuring alone."

"Boss," Météor exclaimed suddenly, "I really want to… but I daren't."

"I can see you coming from here," replied Chantecoq, "you want to ask me a question."

"Boss, there's no hiding anything from you. But don't blame me… it's simply through self-interest and not from curiosity."

"Come on then, out with it."

Météor blurted out, "Boss, I'd like to know what we

ought to say to Slobbis I."

"Slobbis I?"

"Yes, Boris."

"Oh!" Chantecoq replied, "You won't say anything to him."

"Not possible!" the secretary exclaimed, while Landry couldn't hold back a start of surprise.

Chantecoq continued. "You'll give him your letter of convocation which will be signed by him, that's to say this paper that you'll find in its envelope, and simply wait for him to speak to you.

"You're both intelligent enough to know how you'll need to answer him."

"It's just that, boss," objected Météor, "I don't know if my colleague is gifted in financial matters, but as for me, I know absolutely nothing about all that."

"Me neither," declared Landry.

"That doesn't matter," Chantecoq assured them. "Content yourself with doing what I told you and don't worry about the rest. Come on, don't worry about anything. We'll see each other again perhaps sooner than you think!"

"Let's hope so!" Météor concluded.

As he was returning to the laboratory with his colleague, he murmured in Landry's ear, "What he's preparing for us, good God! What's he got in store?"

During this time, Chantecoq was locked deep in his reflections.

Without doubt he was reviewing the plan that he had already established in his mind.

His meditation lasted around half an hour, at the end of which he opened one of his desk drawers and took out a sheet of particularly heavy paper, and personally typed out these few words:

Monsieur Herman Diaz
I shall receive you tomorrow evening, May 28th, at 21:00,
as well as Madame the owner of Petit Sou.

Still using the typewriter, he wrote this address: *Monsieur Herman Diaz, 28 Boulevard Haussman, Paris.*

Then, returning to his desk and keeping Boris's photo in front of him, he signed his letter "Count d'Esseck", imitating Boris's handwriting with a perfection that would have made him the envy of many professional forgers.

He took the envelope, sealed it with the letter inside and then reopened it; then, on the envelope with remarkable skill, he stuck a stamp that he had taken from another letter and which still bore a postmark, illegible however, as happens most of the time. He put the whole thing in a large yellow envelope that he deposited on the table in plain sight and, taking out his watch, he said, "How is it that my son-in-law, who is so punctual, isn't here yet?"

Barely had he uttered those words than the study door opened and a man of around thirty, with a kind, smiling face, eyes which glowed with honesty, and a smile that was naturally benevolent and spiritual, was stepping towards him, hand outstretched.

Chantecoq shook it very cordially, and in a tone of gentle reproach, he said, "I was afraid you might have had an accident."

"Why?"

"Because you're late, my dear."

"Forgive me, but I think that you're mistaken."

"I was expecting you at five o'clock, and it's now five past five."

"For the first time in your life, dear father-in-law," replied Jacques Bellegarde, "you're mistaken! It's two minutes past five. Here's my watch. As it's been around two minutes since I arrived, I therefore got here at the moment that you advised."

"Your watch must be slow."

"I don't think so, perhaps yours is fast."

Chantecoq said, "I have a perfect chronometer; it's not varied by a single second in the year that I've had it."

But as he noticed that the hands were still pointing to five past five, he instinctively put his watch to his ear.

"In the name of the little fellow!" he cried, "It's stopped! This morning, I had so much going on in my head I must have forgotten to rewind it. Forgive me, my dear Jacques. Now, tell me about the mission I entrusted to you and which you've certainly, as always, completed marvellously."

"I don't know if I've completed it marvellously," replied the detective's son-in-law, "but in any case, one thing's for sure, I've fulfilled it with the greatest pleasure, first of all, because I basically like to be useful to you."

"You prove that all the time."

"And also, because this case inspires me."

"Doesn't it, though?"

"What misfortune that I can't, when it's all over and you've claimed yet another victory, recount this adventure to my readers in *Le Petit Parisien*!"

"Unfortunately," declared Chantecoq, "that's impossible, not because of that dreadful Boris whom Météor so picturesquely nicknamed Slobbis I, but because of that poor girl. Although I'm convinced she'll emerge unharmed from this adventure, there are many, if this story were told, who would bang on everywhere that her honour was besmirched.

"Now, I consider that the honour of a young girl is a sacred thing."

"How right you are!" the young journalist exclaimed. "So much more so as we live in an age where too many young girls no longer respect themselves! But there's no point in getting into that delicate subject. You must make haste, dear father-in-law, to learn the information I'm bringing to you."

The meeting between Chantecoq and his son-in-law lasted around quarter of an hour.

When it was finished, Chantecoq was literally radiant.

He said, "I won't pretend that before your arrival, I didn't have a few, if not fears, then a few worries on the path I had chosen. Now, from what you've told me, I'm completely reassured. I can see Boris isn't just a notorious rogue, but also a complete imbecile. That makes things a lot easier! One last question, though. You're sure the signal in question won't be set off before this evening at half past seven?"

"I'm absolutely certain, since I'm the one who has to give it."

"That's what reassures me completely."

"Now we only have one more thing to do, that's to await the moment when the curtain rises on the play's final act."

"Since it's you striking the three blows,[21] I'm sure I won't miss my entrance. Time for a good cigar, my dear Jacques."

Chantecoq presented Bellegarde with a box of Havanas from which he made his choice.

---

[21] It's a convention of French theatre (among others) that the performance starts with three blows (*les trois coups*) struck against the stage with a stick (*le brigadier*) to attract the public's attention. It's a convention much alluded to in French culture: for example at the beginning of Jean-Luc Godard's feature debut *A Bout de Souffle* (1960), where gangster Michel Poiccard (Jean-Paul Belmondo) finds a gun in his stolen car and fires three shots out of the window for no very good reason.

Chantecoq began to fill his pipe, then he asked, "Did you pass by Boulevard de Clichy?"

"I dropped in on my way here."

"Everything's going well?"

"Brilliantly! Gautrais was just arriving and has taken up his post."

"Very good. And Colette?"

"She's your daughter… but she's delighted and very proud to play a part in this business."

"She was remarkable."

"That doesn't surprise me. Meanwhile, allow me to congratulate the great detective of times past and modern for the magisterial fashion with which he set a trap for that Sokovian policeman."

"I assure you," replied Chantecoq, "if poor Madame Gardannes and Mademoiselle Francine's fiancé hadn't been there, the scene would have been the highest comedy. But I think this one won't lack a certain piquancy either."

"I'm depending on you for that," said the journalist. "What a shame I can't be there to witness it!"

"Who's to say that you won't be?"

"I don't see how I can be useful to you."

"Eh! You never know? In any case, if you like and if you're interested… you shall be there, my dear friend…"

"I wonder how you'd be able to get me into the place?"

"Don't you worry about that. But, damn! The time's getting on, since I wound my watch… Follow me to the accessories shop; it's time to take care of our staging."

They both went through to the laboratory, and closed the door behind them.

***

Let's now move to King Boris's office, or rather the Count d'Esseck's office.

Let us pick up at the exact moment where we just left the king of detectives and prince of reporters.

Boris seemed to be in a snappy mood, and in truth he was. That morning, he'd had a long conversation with Arad, who made him aware of the revelations made by Agent Brinquet, whom he had met the night before at the *Ball of the Little White Beds*.

He began by sending out his damned minion with the rudeness which characterised him. But Arad, who knew his master like the back of his hand and knew very well that every time he was given bad news, he worked himself up into an unspeakable fury, waited for the storm to abate.

It lasted around ten minutes, during which several supposed works of art, which decorated the royal office, were thrown across the room by a hand which could no longer restrain itself.

Finally, Boris calmed down and as, when he was calm, he still felt afraid for his life, he said, returning to Arad, who hadn't reacted, "You're not kidding, then?"

"Sire, I swear I spoke the truth."

"Is Brinquet a reliable sort of chap?"

"Sire, I've asked around. I learned that he's one of France's greatest secret agents. That's why I consider it's vital I see this business through, and I'll keep the appointment that he gave me."

"That satanic Barbara," hissed the king in fury, "that one's going to make life difficult for me. Ah! If I could only procure, not proof she wants to murder me, but which would be much more important, to recover those secret documents that I stupidly allowed her to steal. Oh! Then I wouldn't hesitate for a moment to drag her before a court or make her vanish, without anyone ever learning what became of her."

"Which would be infinitely preferable," added Arad, who didn't seem to nurture any particular affection for his king's favourite.

The king replied, "Unfortunately, that's impossible!"

"Permit me to respectfully observe to Your Majesty that, until now, we've directed barely any attention in that direction. Your Majesty gave me the formal order to take care of Madame the Duchess de Castrovillari and Your Majesty knows that I'd never wish to exceed his will. But, in my humble opinion, I believe it's time to act."

"How would you manage that?"

Arad explained, "Once I've obtained, thanks to Agent Brinquet, the confession of the duchess's accomplice, it will be easy to intimidate that girl. As she must certainly have very close links to the duchess, perhaps I'll manage to find out where the documents are hidden, and seize them.

"Your Majesty will only have to give me the list of them and he can be certain that all those papers will be loyally returned to him by my hand. I will then have the joy, honour, and pride to have assured my King's peace of mind."

"To me this all seems interesting and very well-reasoned," replied the sovereign, "so follow the case in the sense I indicated to you. Take care for example…"

"Sire, I don't know who Barbara's accomplice is, but I'll know soon, and I'll immediately let Your Majesty know."

Boris replied. "It certainly can't be the first to come. In any case, one thing I'm sure of, is that the duchess is a highly astute woman and one of the most dangerous vipers one might meet on one's path. She's the sort you can't crush under your heel, they always manage to bite you first!"

And he concluded, "Be on your guard and keep me updated, as soon as you've carried out your first operation. I've no other advice to give you. You certainly know your job as a policeman better than I know mine as a king. I'll add, however, that yours is much more difficult…"

"Sire!" Arad protested, solely for form's sake, because deep down, he absolutely shared the judgement that the unworthy king had just pronounced on himself with so much glibness.

After having bowed before Boris, he went to camouflage himself, as we've already seen, ahead of his meeting with Chantecoq, of which we already know the outcome; lamentable for the Sokovian, and triumphant for our hero.

Following this meeting the amorous ogre had remained highly perplexed. He wondered, indeed, if things were going to turn out so favourably as the chief of his secret police had assured him.

As he said to Arad, Barbara was one of those dreadful women who, he'd just had further proof of it, stopped at nothing in order to sate their passion and their appetites.

We saw, elsewhere, that Boris was far from personifying courage and we might even say rather that he was something of a poltroon. Knowing himself to be under constant threat from that woman made him experience a feeling which was more than nausea… but fear.

But, held by the threats she had dangled before him, he always recoiled from extreme measures and, more and more, he expected to be the victim of that woman whom he hadn't the resources to have assassinated.

And now the chief of his secret police was bringing him, thanks to an obliging French agent, the means to be done, once and for all, with that woman whom he once if not loved, but at the very least violently desired, and whom he

185

now considered to be nothing but a sort of female demon, bent on his downfall.

That restored his courage a bit and, naturally, having cursed that damned woman once more, he directed his thoughts towards the little French girl who was so delicious, so seductive, who was resting under his roof, quite nearby, and whom, since the drama which had unfolded in front of him, he hadn't dared visit.

So, after several moments of hesitation, attracted, despite himself, by that delicious being, so different to those courtesans, of whom he'd made real queens, and to those duchesses, of whom he'd made courtesans, he stood, left his office quietly through a small door which led to his bedroom and, from there, headed towards a vast double wardrobe of a very modern style, which stood against the wall opposite his bed.

He opened the wardrobe's two doors. It was empty and contained no shelves.

He pressed his finger against a knothole placed in the middle of the back of the wardrobe: the panel swung open and revealed the back of a second wardrobe, also empty, which the king entered. Pushing a special lock, he opened its doors and poked his head through the gap.

Lying in a bed with sky blue hangings and bright white sheets, Francine was sleeping peacefully, after the ardent fever of the first days.

She had finally found relaxation and oblivion in sleep.

Just as Arad had said to Chantecoq, the young girl had been very well cared for by the king's private physician, a practitioner who was devoid of all scruples, concerned only with money, but knowing his profession for all that.

The king, quietly, closed the wardrobe and, on tiptoes, approached the bed.

"She's both beautiful and pretty, all at once!" he murmured, contemplating the adorable face with its slightly pale complexion, its eyes with slight dark circles and forehead framed by those pretty golden curls, which looked so much like a halo.

Slowly, Francine's eyelids cracked open. She didn't recognise her abductor at once and this gentle word, the first on the lips of all young people in pain, slipped from her slightly discoloured lips, "Mother... mother!"

No doubt she thought her mother was there.

She had barely come out of her slumber, she must be continuing a dream, because, reaching out, she said in a voice which was still broken, "You're there, aren't you, darling?"

And she added, "And Robert? Has he returned from Rouen?"

Sudden rage turned the Count d'Esseck's face purple. Jealousy had bitten him. Those simple words, almost unconscious, escaping from that virginal mouth, sufficed to make him understand that, if it was still within his power to seize this young woman, be it, by necessity, through force, or through cunning, she would belong to him, but never of her own consent; and would only ever be a beautiful slave who would defend herself tirelessly against his dreadful embrace.

So, he moved even closer. He dared to speak.

"Mademoiselle," he said, "don't be afraid. You're among friends here."

Suddenly returning to her senses, Francine sat up, recognising her gaoler. Her eyes widened with sudden dread, she tried to push the atrocious vision away with her trembling hands, as he moved closer towards her and seemed to be trying to envelop her, to carry her away.

Boris, with a hypocritical and gentle voice, continued. "Don't be scared, I repeat, I'm your friend."

"No, no," Robert's fiancée was revolted, "you're a monster... yes, a monster...

"I don't want to see you or to hear you. Let me go... if not, as soon as I have the strength, I'll throw myself from the window again and, this time, I'll kill myself, because, after the shame you've inflicted on me, the only thing left is death."

"My dear child," replied the wretch, "you won't do that, first, because as you can see through the gap in the curtains, your windows are protected by bars, which your charming wrists and delicate hands won't manage to remove. And then, death... why? I ask you."

"I just told you."

"That's madness..."

Maintaining his sly, perfidiously persuasive attitude, Boris continued. "I'm the first to acknowledge I acted towards you with a brutality for which I beg you to accept my apologies.

"But the passion you inspired in me reached such paroxysms that I was no longer in control of my actions. I had lost my head completely. How can I obtain your pardon?"

"Return me to my family," retorted Francine, with an energy that her kidnapper would never have suspected from her.

A little disconcerted by that response, which proved that the young girl was even more immovable, Boris replied, "My God! Mademoiselle, I'm not saying no... I'm not the sort of person to keep people by force who don't want to stay. But as I already told you, and allow me to repeat it, you're setting aside the greatest opportunity for happiness that a woman could find in life."

"I could never be happy," cried Francine, "I think I already told you, too. No, I'd never be happy with anyone other than he who has already won my heart completely!"

"Listen to me!"

"You won't manage to make me change my mind. You're rich, very rich, your power is great, perhaps greater than I imagined, because, now I come to think about it: for you to dare to carry out in Paris such a disgusting, cowardly act as the one of which I'm the victim, you must not have much to fear from my country's justice!"

Boris, anxious to display his influence and authority, retorted in a tone which he attempted to make sound majestic.

"The fact is you're an excessively interesting young girl and I greatly admire you for reasoning like this at a time when your soul is so troubled. I am indeed powerful, very powerful, and I'm sheltered, as you've guessed, from any intrusion from the French police into my private life.

"On the other hand, I possess all the means which ought to convince a woman, whoever she is, to abandon the poor scrap of joy that she dreamed of on this earth, in order to link her destiny, even outside legal bonds, to a person who rules several million subjects, who is at the head of a mighty army, who is allied to France, in one word: *A KING!*"

Boris was counting greatly on this emphasis to impress Francine and make her more favourable to his designs. He produced the opposite effect.

Staring the wretch in the eye, her own full of limpid and angelic frankness, she said, "You're a king, monsieur, and you conduct yourself like this!"

"A king is a man like any other," retorted the Count d'Esseck.

"No, not when he acts as you've acted towards me, because, happily, there are few men who would dare to attack a young girl in such a cowardly fashion, to drown a mother in

189

anguish and to bring despair to the heart of a loving and beloved fiancé.

"You knew all that, you knew all about my life. Ah! I'm now convinced: to achieve your aims, as you have done, you must have been fully informed about me; you must have known I'm an honest girl, that all I wanted in life were the joys found in selfless love and sincere art.

"You've trampled over all of that, you destroyed everything, wrecked everything, and you wanted to make everything wither: my soul, my body, my love, my hopes, my ambitions. And you still imagine that, because you told me you're a powerful king, that you rule over several million subjects, command an imposing army, that you're in possession of a considerable fortune, that you wanted to make me your favourite, I would break with a past which is all my honour and all my pride, to fall in your arms like a girl who sells herself, instead of a lover who gives herself!"

"Come now!" cried the king, pale with rage and disappointment.

"Don't add another word, monsieur," said Francine, "I guess your intentions only too well not to tell you about my own. You want to keep me prisoner, because you hope to wear me out and vanquish me through lassitude, through boredom! Don't have that hope; if you won't set me free, or if you have the misfortune to touch me, I swear on my mother's head that I'll go on hunger strike, that I'll swallow no solid or liquid food.

"I'll take perhaps fifteen days, three weeks to die. Maybe longer, but I'll certainly die. I don't know if you believe in anything, I don't think so. A man such as you, however highly-placed, can have convictions of command and accomplish only official acts of faith.

"I, without being pious, am a believer and, while

190

admitting that down here there's no innate justice, especially for those who, like you, are placed in such a way that they can defy it with impunity, I call on God's judgement!

"Remember, if you know your French history... Remember that, while the Templars burned on the pyre that Philip the Fair built for them[22], their master, their leader, Jacques Molay,[23] gave testimony before the divine tribunal, to the King of France after a delay of six weeks which followed their ordeal. Six weeks later, Philip the Fair expired."

"I was unaware of that legend," the King of Sokovia tried to joke.

"It's not a legend," replied Francine, "it's the truth."

"Oh! The truth…"

Mademoiselle Gardannes, whose gaze still gleamed with fever, cried out, "Whatever it was, remember this, *monsieur*: you hold my liberty and my life in your hands. You're responsible for both one and the other and remember that I prefer death to prison!"

Those last words, spoken with a sort of divine inspiration, made a certain impression on the King of Sokovia.

He said to himself, "She's a little fanatic and she's perfectly capable of pulling a hunger strike on me, just as she threatened. The best thing is not to insist. This evening, I'll telephone Doctor Troesco to come by tomorrow morning and I'll see what he advises."

Aloud he replied, cautiously, "Mademoiselle, I won't

---

[22] Philippe IV of France, AKA Philippe le Bel (1285-1314). The bit that Francine doesn't mention is that Philippe suppressed the Knights Templar largely because he owed them substantial amounts of money.

[23] Jacques de Molay (1243-1314). The last Grand Master of the Knights Templar, no matter what various Dan Brown novels or Assassin's Creed games might have you believe.

insist, I'm going to reflect. Perhaps I will grant your wish."

"Then," cried Mademoiselle Gardannes, "all will be forgiven for you."

"We'll see, we'll see," said the king, imitating, doubtless unaware, the evasive fashion with which Louis XIV[24] responded to requests which displeased or embarrassed him.

After having bowed to his victim, instead of going through the wardrobe, he left through a door, which led to a corridor and to which he alone had the key. He returned to his office.

"Decidedly," he said to himself, "these Frenchwomen have extraordinary bravery. They all have a Joan of Arc who sleeps in their hearts and who wakes as soon as they believe themselves to be in danger. After all, it would be daft on my part, after risking so much, to send this pretty girl back home, particularly as, so far, I don't think the alarm has been raised. The best thing to do is be patient and wait.

"Sweetness is better than violence, as said I don't know which poet of this country.[25]

"All in all, perhaps he was right, and if I reined in my ardour a little, it's probable that I would have managed to overcome this lovely bird's resistance much sooner."

During this time, hours had passed and Boris, who had completely forgotten about Arad, suddenly remembered him.

Consulting the board hanging from one of his office

---

[24] Louis XIV (1638-1715). AKA Louis the Great, AKA The Sun King, Louis was King of France from 1643 until 1715, making him the longest-reigning monarch in European history (Holy Roman Empire notwithstanding).

[25] *Probably* Jean de la Fontaine (1621-1695), but could be Edouard Pailleron (1834-1899), or a couple of others. I don't know, King Boris doesn't know, and frankly I doubt Arthur Bernède had much idea either.

walls, he said to himself, "He ought to be back already. I know all too well with these police adventures, you never know quite where they might lead those who are mixed up in them."

He looked out of his window and said, "The weather's nice, I'm going to go for a drive."

He rang. A lackey appeared. Boris said to him, "Warn Monsieur Rupert de Rurick that we're going out shortly."

He went into his bathroom, put on a sports jacket, with his valet's help; then he returned to his office where he already found Count Rupert.

He had a sad, prim face. At once, Boris guessed that he was the bearer of bad news.

After having hailed his master, according to the rules of protocol, the counsellor began.

"I apologise for being forced to communicate to Your Majesty a message which just reached me."

Rurick held out to his master an unsealed telegram which he held in his hand.

"Read it, read it yourself," ordered the sovereign in an annoyed voice.

Rurick read the dispatch aloud, which was composed as follows:

Count Mardeck seriously injured in a car accident. Doctors are not yet giving out any information. Please warn His Majesty, whose presence seems to be crucial in our capital.

"Goodness me!" cried Boris. "That is, indeed, very irritating news; all I need would be to lose my Prime Minister! A man who carries out my business so well and thanks to whom I don't need to concern myself with anything, other than presiding over some vague official ceremonies from time to time. As of now, I renounce my trip in the car. You go and get a telephone connection to Sokovia at once! I need to have the details reported in person!"

"Sire, I'm on my way to the direct line."

"That's it, don't talk so much. You ought to have left already."

Baron Rupert hurried to dash out. Boris began to pace his office, nervous.

"What a day," he said. "Barbara wants to murder me! That little Parisian girl is almost turning down a throne and my Prime Minister has crashed into a ditch!

"If things go on like this, then farewell, Sokovia! I'll cash in my fortune, I'll abdicate, and I'll proclaim a Republic in my nation. I don't want to be the sucker that most conventional monarchs are. So, they can have a dictator, or Bolsheviks... I don't care. After all, that will perhaps be a sport just as agreeable as many others."

But King Boris hadn't reached the end of his surprises, or his worries. The day which was ending was going to count among the most unpleasant of his life. Indeed, he soon saw his counsellor return, looking ashen with shock.

"You were able to obtain communication?" Boris asked.

"Yes, sire."

"And?"

Bowing, Baron Rupert revealed, "Monsieur the Count de Mardeck just expired."

An oath burst from the unworthy king's lips.

Then he thundered, "What did he need to do that for, to get himself demolished just when I needed him? Quite apart from the fact he was very popular and he was doing whatever he wanted with my subjects. With him, you didn't have to fear a tile might fall on your head. So, we'll have to go."

"Sire, I think that's absolutely necessary," declared Rupert de Rurick. "The Orient Express leaves tomorrow morning, but I think that Your Majesty, instead of taking that mode of transport, would do better to leave by aeroplane."

"What are you talking about? Me, get into such a device! Oh! So you want me to end up like my Prime Minister?"

"Sire, Your Majesty is going to force me to tell him certain things…"

"But tell me, my friend, tell me… What's stopping you?"

"Count Mardeck's secretary, who gave me the sad news, added that several corteges are circulating around the city, chanting, 'Down with King Boris! Long live the Republic!'"

"They can chant whatever they want, the idiots. It's only a matter of sending out a few tanks into the streets and you'll soon see those brawlers hide in their cellars."

"The problem is that a large portion of the army has moved over to the demonstrators' side."

"Oh well! Have that part of the army shot by the rest of them. Everything will be fine."

"Sire, Your Majesty alone has the right to take such a decision and, also, is alone in having the necessary authority to quell the rebellion."

"But then, Monsieur Counsellor," shouted the unbearable rogue, "do you imagine I'm going to wedge myself into this wasps' nest? Not on your life… if they want nothing more to do with me, I want nothing more to do with them. I agreed to be king on the condition I was spared all responsibility and all worries. Now things are turning out badly, it's my turn to go on strike. I'm fine here, I'm staying put!"

"But Her Majesty the queen?" objected Baron Rupert, barely able to hide his indignation.

"The queen? No one will dare touch her. And moreover she's surrounded by friends, she knows where to go... the British consul is there. After all, she is an English princess."

Consternated, Rupert fell silent.

He was a rather sad specimen himself, but next to the disgusting spectacle provided by his sovereign, he felt despite himself that his heart was flinching in disgust and, to put an end to this pathetic scene, he said, "Your Majesty will do as it best pleases him."

He was going to withdraw, when a telephone rang.

Rupert tried to grab the device, but the Count d'Esseck stopped him with an authoritative gesture and, nervously took up the receiver, into which he said, "Hello! Who's there?"

"Arad," said a voice on the other end of the line.

"Ah! It's you at last."

"Sire," explained a voice which couldn't be Arad's, since he was Chantecoq's prisoner, "I have at hand the proof of everything I told you yesterday.

"If you'd like to come and meet me at the Chateau d'Orbois, I think that not only will I prove that I didn't lie to you, but I'll furnish the necessary evidence to Your Majesty to condemn the person that you know and to remove all the weapons that she threatens to make use of."

"Good work!" replied the king, a little reassured by this message which, according to all appearances, was going to give him the possibility of ridding himself of a favourite who had become more than compromising.

And turning to his counsellor, who hadn't moved, he said, "We're going to pay Barbara a little visit which she's hardly expecting; but I believe you're going to witness, my dear Rupert, a scene such as you'll not have seen in your whole life."

"What a day!" cried the counsellor, wiping his forehead. "I truly fear it's going to end, not in drama but in tragedy."

A few minutes later, King Boris sped off in his car, which he was driving himself, in the direction of Bois de Boulogne.

How great was the porter's astonishment when, around an hour later, he saw the king return, alone at the wheel.

"Probably," he said to himself, "he had to drop off the counsellor on the way."

He hastened to open the entrance gates, then watched the king carry out a smart turn, which brought him before the steps, on which the lackey had just appeared, who was rushing towards his master in order to open the car door for him.

Boris, who was more and more nervous, launched himself on to the steps which he climbed at an accelerated pace. Entering the house like a gust of wind, he climbed the grand staircase and went straight to his office, the door to which he slammed loudly.

The lackeys, who had wind of the Sokovian Revolution were watching him, shaking their heads. One simply said, "He doesn't look happy."

The other, more severe, added, "It's no more than he deserves."

Quarter of an hour later, two people presented themselves at the gate. One had all the appearance of a wealthy Argentine, the other had the classic appearance of a businesswoman, such as we see occasionally and who don't always have the good fortune to succeed in their financial operations.

They spoke to the porter, who came out to them, and made him aware of a typed letter which bore the signature of His Majesty, the King of Sokovia.

There's no use hiding it: our readers will certainly have

recognised, in the two visitors, Chantecoq's two secretaries: Paul Landry and Météor.

The document they held bore signs of the most careful authenticity.

The porter didn't hesitate to show in the director of the International Bank of Europe and Asia, and the publisher of the *Gazette du Petit Sou*, to the hallway where the ordinary lackeys were mounting guard.

The director and the publisher showed one of them the letter of introduction, with which they were armed.

At once, very politely, he showed them into a waiting room and went to warn, as was his duty, the policeman Mako, who was waiting in a ground floor room and who had the mission, that evening, of watching over his master's safety particularly closely.

Mako, who had received strict instructions, went to the room where Météor and Landry were waiting.

As soon as he had taken a good look at them, he interrogated them on the reason for their visit.

The two young bloodhounds, who were playing their roles marvellously, answered that they had been introduced to King Boris by an influential French politician, former minister, president of the commission, etc, etc, and that His Majesty, very interested by the propositions that both of them had made him, had summoned them, that evening, with a view to talking constructively.

Mako, although in the same profession, didn't detect, in either of his visitors, two colleagues, who were certainly more gifted than he was, if only in the highly tricky art of camouflage.

Aware of his sovereign's state of mind and suspecting, following the news from his capital, that he might not be precisely in the mood to discuss stock market operations, he paused.

"I don't know if Monsieur the Count d'Esseck, although he made an appointment with you, will be able to receive you, because he has been taken with a sudden indisposition. He left in the car and had to return very swiftly."

"Please tell him that we're here in any case," Météor squeaked in a screechy voice, which was worthy of figuring among those which, every day, let out piercing cries, and prolonged vociferation along the courtyards of our national Stock Exchange.

"After all," Mako said to himself, "what am I risking, with a man as whimsical as Boris? He's perfectly capable of blaming me for having kicked out these two people."

And he replied aloud, "Wait here. I'll go and see if His Majesty will deign to receive you."

"Oh, he'll deign," said the fake bank director with magisterial aplomb.

Mako went to knock at the king's door. A groan answered him. Interpreting that as meaning "Come in!" the policeman entered the office and found his master with his head in his hands. Mako, who feared a violent storm, began timidly.

"Sire, there are two people here who gave me this letter signed by Your Majesty, in which an appointment has been fixed by you."

Boris, while keeping his head leaning on his palm, read the letter that Arad's colleague handed to him; he browsed it distractedly and ordered, in a hoarse voice, "Send them up."

Mako left, saying to himself, "I had a lucky instinct, not kicking those two out."

A few moments later, he returned with them to the royal office.

Boris, who still seemed prostrate in deep meditation, sent the agent away with a curt gesture.

Without moving, and without even asking the director and the publisher to sit down, he said to them, "Now, tell me what you want."

Météor and Landry exchanged a rather anxious glance.

They looked like two students who were taking their baccalaureat, and they were getting ready to dry up majestically in front of their examiner.

"Come on, then! Speak!" Boris insisted.

Météor, who had more gumption than his colleague, began, in a voice which seemed to have been borrowed from a cantor in the Sistine Chapel.

"It's a matter of the gold deposits in the lands of…"

Suddenly, the king shouted, "Spare me the gold deposits and go and bolt that door."

"Boss!" Météor exclaimed, puffing out his cheeks fit to make them burst.

"Ah! You're not going to pretend you didn't recognise me!" the king of detectives exclaimed, while Météor carried out the order his boss had given him with his usual speed.

"Boss, I swear on the head that I hold dearest in the world, that's to say your own, after my own… yes, I swear that I, even though I'm used to seeing you transform yourself into a hundred different people, this time, I didn't have a clue. And you, Landry?"

"Me," declared his colleague, "I would have bet a hundred that I was facing the King of Sokovia."

"Now, my children, that we're in place, it's time to make the most of it, although I've nothing to fear from Slobbis I, who, when he wakes up, will find himself lying in the same bed as his loyal Arad. I consider we must put everything at stake in order to free Mademoiselle Gardannes. Therefore, what it remains for us to do, is to discover the bedroom where she's hidden.

"That ought not to be too difficult; because I've already carried out an external reconnaissance, which, with the bit of topography with which you furnished me, my brave Météor, allowed me to reconstitute almost exactly the layout of the place, at the same time as the placing of the bedrooms. For my money, Mademoiselle Gardannes must be in a room adjoining the king's bedroom, whose windows garnished with thick bars look out over the garden.

"The reason I'm firm in this conviction is that none of the other windows are barred; it's one thing of which Boris and his accomplices hadn't thought, but it didn't escape me. The area for our research is therefore extremely circumscribed. On the other hand, Boris's bedroom must communicate directly with the bedroom where he's sequestered Monsieur Robert Santenois's fiancée. The first thing to do is to get into Boris's bedchamber."

Météor declared, "I think I can declare without risk of error, boss, that the door you see there, opposite the chimney, leads straight there."

"I'm going," Chantecoq decided immediately. "As for you, stay there, but come running only at my call; because we must avoid attracting the attention of the police and the stooges, who must be present here in rather large numbers. So, careful! Keep your eyes and ears open and, above all, avoid the slightest slip-up."

Météor wasn't mistaken: the door he had indicated indeed led to the royal chamber.

Chantecoq entered; the first thing he did was close the interior bolt of the door which led to the corridor which served the whole first floor.

He went to open another; it led to a bathroom which had no other exit. He went to the window; he inched it open gently and leaned slightly outside.

He hadn't been mistaken: the neighbouring window, on his right, as well as the one next to that, was covered by the solid iron bars he had noticed from outside.

"So far," he said, "this isn't going too badly. But, contrary to my suppositions, I don't believe there's a direct passage between this room and the other, unless Boris put in a secret entrance. But where? There's the problem. I can't demolish the wall with a pickaxe; first, I lack the principal tool in question, and I believe it would be quite difficult to make use of one without attracting the staff's attention."

He began to pace the room, sniffing the air like a true bloodhound, examining the paintings, the furnishings which decorated the room, when his attention paused over the great wardrobe which took up a considerable amount of space and seemed, at first glance, absolutely inoffensive. He approached it and examined the lock, which seemed quite complex.

"Damn!" he thought, "Am I going to find in my pouch the key I need to open this monument which must contain other things than clothes and linen?"

He drew from his pocket the pouch to which he had just alluded and which held around fifty keys in strange shapes, some of which resembled crochet hooks, and even fishhooks.

He took a long look at the lock, chose a hook, placed it in a small wooden sleeve that he had also taken out of his pocket and began his work with a precision, method, and patience that our most selective and most refined modern burglars don't always have.

He was rewarded for his effort because, after around ten minutes, the two panels opened and revealed the interior of the furniture to be completely empty; which rather indicated that it was solely serving to hide the passage that the king of detectives sought.

He found himself facing a single panel which bore no trace of a lock.

Chantecoq didn't doubt for a moment that there was some form of secret mechanism there.

But where was this mechanism?

He really would have struggled to say.

Through sheer obstinacy, it was highly possible he'd discover it, but that was going to require time, and Chantecoq needed to act fast.

He gave the wall a few thumps, which made a heavy, stifled sound, indicating that it must be armoured internally, which thwarted all hope of managing to open it by other means.

"Quite a snag!" Chantecoq murmured.

At once, with his usual optimism, he continued. "But a snag because it's a dead end. We must expect, however, to run into some obstacles. I've known others, this isn't enough to frighten me.

"Meanwhile, I'm going to rejoin our two lads, who must certainly be wondering what's going on and must be anxious, as much as I am, to know how things are going to turn out."

He returned by the same path to Boris's office. Météor and Landry hadn't moved.

Chantecoq said to them, "I've spotted the exact room where Mademoiselle Gardannes is located. Only, I've encountered some difficulty getting in. I just found myself, indeed, faced with the door to a vault, which I don't think I can manage without a great deal of time and effort.

Météor exclaimed, "Boss, what if I went down the chimney?"

"I was thinking about that," replied Chantecoq, "but I decided on it only if I can't do anything else. I don't want to expose you to a futile effort, and perhaps danger. Let's see, let's think a bit. This individual who let you both in earlier, he must know! Hide in the bedroom, I'm going to ring, he'll come and then, willingly or by force, he'll show me what we came looking for."

At that moment, there was a knock at the door.

Chantecoq, who was very close to it, pulled back the bolt softly; then, returning to his desk on tiptoes, he said, "Come in!"

Mako appeared, announcing with a mysterious air, "Doctor Troesco has come, Your Majesty, to take care of You Know What."

Chantecoq said to himself, "This is definitely my chance, this doctor must be the one who, from what Arad told me, has practised his care on Mademoiselle Gardannes. Come on, everything's going great!"

Aloud, he said to the old director and to the fake publisher, "Forgive me for interrupting our terribly interesting conversation; but I'm obliged to receive my physician."

And addressing Mako, he ordered, "Show this gentleman and this lady into the lounge. As soon as I ring, bring them back in."

Mako took Météor and Landry into the lounge next door to the office; then he went to fetch Troesco and brought him to the man he was continuing to mistake for his sovereign.

When he had closed the door behind the visitor, Chantecoq resumed the meditative attitude that he adopted at the beginning of this scene and which also managed to hide his face completely from the visitor's attention.

He made a simple gesture to the doctor to sit down. Troesco, who was Sokovian, spoke a few words in his own language, of which Chantecoq naturally didn't understand a blessed word.

The king of detectives told himself that all conversation was pointless and that the moment had come to hurry things along. In one bound he jumped up like an uncoiling spring and, brandishing a revolver, he said to him in French, "Hands up right now! Take me immediately to the young girl who's locked up in this house."

Troesco, convinced he was in the presence of the Count d'Esseck, collapsed, literally petrified and murmured between his teeth, which were chattering with fright, "The king has gone mad!"

"No," declared Chantecoq, "I'm not mad. I know what I'm saying as well as I know what I want. If, in two minutes, you've not decided to obey me, I'm using the contents of your skull to make as lovely a dish of sautéed brains such as I've never yet seen on a restaurant menu."

"He's mad, my God he's mad! He's going to kill me!" the doctor lamented.

"So, you don't want to get going?" snarled the great bloodhound, more and more threatening.

"But, sire, since only you know the wardrobe's secret and only you have the key to the other door, how do you want me to get you into that room?"

Chantecoq, who never let himself be flummoxed, retorted, "The mechanism is broken and I've lost the key! But, in fact, now I think about… yes… that's it…"

And still threatening the unfortunate Troesco with his Browning, the king of detectives added, in a tone which brooked no reply, "Walk ahead of me up to the door of the little one's bedroom. Anyway, we have a score to settle in the presence of Mademoiselle Gardannes, of whom you've told me a whole bunch of stories…"

"I, sire? I would never have permitted myself to…"

"Walk ahead, I tell you!"

And pressing on a buzzer, he said to Mako, who had appeared at once and was also wondering if his king hadn't suddenly lost his mind, "Fetch the gentleman and the lady who are in the lounge and bring them to my room."

"To your room, sire?"

"To my room, idiot!"

Mako said to himself, "That's it… the last straw. Nothing like a revolution to overthrow a king…"

Nevertheless, he obeyed at once, because the revolver with which the fake Boris was playing was enough to make him carry out all his master's wishes with diligence.

Chantecoq rejoined the doctor who was waiting for him in the doorway, in the corridor which led to the royal bedchamber.

Chantecoq was fixed; and aiming a huge kick at Troesco's backside, he said to him, "I've seen enough of you now, get out of here, and get yourself hanged elsewhere."

Troesco didn't need telling twice. He left quickly, tumbling down the stairs and announcing to all the staff who had come running, "The king is having a full breakdown; don't try to approach him. He's armed… there would certainly be a mishap. I'm running to police headquarters to fetch some agents, who, armed with shields and tear gas, will certainly manage to subdue this furious madman."

Meanwhile, Chantecoq was not wasting any time.

He selected from his pouch not a hook, but a key which slipped instantly into the lock without the slightest difficulty, and the door opened.

Mademoiselle Gardannes who, just as she had declared to the amorous ogre, had refused to eat even the slightest food, was lying on her bed.

At the sight of he whom she assumed to be Boris, she froze. Chantecoq said, stepping towards her, "Calm yourself,

206

mademoiselle. Although I bear an enormous resemblance to the wretch who tried to dishonour you, I don't even have the shame of being his brother.

"I am, quite simply, Chantecoq, a detective. I promised your mother and your fiancé to bring you back safe and sound. It's done. You've nothing more to fear from the King of Sokovia and, if you want, I'll take you to your fiancé at once. He's nearby, awaiting you with keen impatience."

"Is this possible?" Francine exclaimed. "I'm not dreaming?"

"No, mademoiselle, you're wide awake. I'm going to withdraw for a moment, so you can put on the coat I see lying on the chair over there; and I'll then ask you to leave this house on my arm, so long as you feel strong enough to take a few steps. If not, I'll carry you swiftly towards the happiness that awaits you."

While speaking, Chantecoq, so as to convince Francine, had taken off the fake moustache and the wig, thanks to which he had succeeded, by adding careful make-up, to reconstitute the features of the man that Météor called Slobbis I.

Transfigured, galvanised by the new force that was bringing her the certainty of her liberation, Francine cried out, "Yes, in five minutes, Monsieur Chantecoq, come back. It's on your arm, indeed, that I want to leave this house."

Chantecoq went quickly to find Météor and Landry, who were waiting in the king's bedchamber.

"Now," he said, "Success is certain. Both of you dash off to announce the good news to Monsieur Santenois, who's waiting for us in a car, not thirty metres from here."

Météor replied, "Boss, you're not worried that…"

"I fear nothing," cried Chantecoq, "with the little toy I have here, in my hands."

While his two secretaries dashed off, Chantecoq went to knock on the door to Francine's room.

She opened it herself. She'd put on her travelling clothes and wore a pair of slippers on her feet.

"Now, Monsieur Chantecoq," she said, "I'm ready to follow you."

They reached the main staircase; but there, things were about to unravel.

Indeed, as soon as they saw Francine Gardannes walking on the arm not of King Boris, but of a man with a strange face, red cheeks and features streaked with black, all the household staff understood they had been tricked and that the woman, whom their master had guarded so jealously, was being taken away.

"Never fear," murmured Chantecoq in Francine's ear, as she had taken a step back. "I'll kill them all, but there won't be a single one of them dead."

And, suiting his actions to his words, he fired his revolver at Mako who, the first, was climbing the staircase. Mako twirled on himself, and, grabbing the banister, let himself fall to the hallway's tiled floor, collapsed, annihilated, which had the result of making all the others flee.

Quickly, Chantecoq led the young girl on, saying, "They're not very brave, the servants of Slobbis I. To flee like that before a revolver loaded with blanks, it really is a mark of cowardice!"

And, without giving the policeman time to get a grip on himself, as well as the stooges who were hidden wherever they could find, Chantecoq and Francine stepped outside.

The detective, crossing the garden, had the gate opened, threatening the porter with the same inoffensive revolver. Two minutes later, Francine, broken with emotion and with joy, was swooning in her fiancé's arms. But she didn't take long to come round and, noticing her saviour, who was looking at her with a paternal expression, she said, "Where are you taking me now?"

Chantecoq answered. "To your mother, who's expecting you and who will be so happy to realise that her dreadful nightmare has ended!"

We won't describe the joy of Madame Gardannes when, after being warned by her future son-in-law, with all necessary care, that her daughter was saved, Francine threw herself into her arms.

"My Francine, my beloved child!"

This was all the poor mother could say.

At length, she held against her chest the daughter that she had truly feared she would never see again.

"My darling," cried the young girl, "I always hoped... I was always convinced that I would survive this dreadful adventure unharmed. What overwhelmed me above all, was the thought that you and my dear Robert, you were both plunged into sorrow and anguish."

Madame Gardannes, comforted, replied, "Robert has been wonderful. It was he who had the idea of consulting the private detective Chantecoq."

"An admirable man!" Francine breathed.

And addressing her fiancé, she added, "The challenge we've just overcome has further strengthened the links which already bound us. Robert, now, I'm sure of it, we'll be happy, happier than we ever imagined, perhaps..."

"Francine," replied the young engineer, "You are and you always will be my whole life."

Reaching her trembling hands towards them, Madame Gardannes murmured, "And I, my children, I bless you!"

***

Let's leave Madame Gardannes, Francine and Robert Santenois to their deserved joy. And let's return to Chantecoq.

The king of detectives who, helped by his son-in-law and Robert Santenois, had succeeded in drawing Boris into an ambush by telephoning him under Arad's name and asking him to come and meet at the Chateau d'Arbois, after having let Baron Rupert run away, had given the amorous ogre the same injection as the chief of secret police and then asked Bellegarde to take him to Boulevard de Clichy. But he didn't intend for the amorous ogre and his accomplice to remain at his children's house any longer. He simply asked Landry and Météor to go and dump the king and the chief of his secret police on a bench on the boulevard, where they continued to sleep until the police noticed them and took care of them.

The following day, one could read in the newspapers the following note, which plunged Paris, France and the whole world into the most complete stupefaction; it was composed thus:

While the Sokovian people, following the death of Count Mardeck, were revolting against royal authority, and while the unfortunate queen of Sokovia succeeded in fleeing only thanks to the devotion of her courageous servants, King Boris I and the head of his secret police were found dead drunk on a bench in a boulevard.

At the time of writing, this sad monarch has still not come out of his torpor.

Indeed, he only came out of it after forty-eight hours, to receive full punishment for his crimes.

Duchess Barbara de Castrovillari managed to poison him

a few days later, just as she had threatened on several occasions; but, betrayed by her accomplice, none other than the policeman Mako, she was arrested two days later.

The two culprits appeared before the Assizes court, where they were sentenced, she, to perpetual imprisonment, and he to twenty years of public service.

As to Robert Santenois and Francine, they now knew complete happiness, which had failed to elude them.

At the point where we end this tale, we learn from the very mouth of our dear friend Chantecoq that it will not be long before he becomes a godfather!

FIN

CHANTECOQ AND MÉTÉOR WILL RETURN IN…

CHANTECOQ AND THE
PÈRE-LACHAISE GHOST

ABOUT THE AUTHOR

Arthur Bernède (5 January 1871 – 20 March 1937) was a French writer, poet, opera librettist, and playwright.

Bernède was born in Redon, Ille-et-Vilaine department, in Brittany. In 1919, Bernède joined forces with actor René Navarre, who had played Fantômas in the Louis Feuillade serials, and writer Gaston Leroux, the creator of Rouletabille, to launch the Société des Cinéromans, a production company that would produce films and novels simultaneously. Bernède published almost 200 adventure, mystery, and historical novels. His best-known characters are Belphégor, Judex, Mandrin, Chantecoq, and Vidocq. Bernède also collaborated on plays, poems, and opera libretti with Paul de Choudens; including several operas by Félix Fourdrain.

Bernède also wrote the libretti for a number of operas, among them Jules Massenet's Sapho and Camille Erlanger's L'Aube rouge.

ABOUT THE TRANSLATOR

Andrew Lawston grew up in rural Hampshire, where he later worked for a short time as a French teacher. He moved to London to work in magazine publishing, alongside pursuing his interests in writing, translation, and acting.

In addition to translating the chronicles of Chantecoq for the English-speaking world, Andrew has written a number of science-fiction and urban fantasy books, full of his particular brand of humour. Andrew currently lives in West London with his lovely wife Mel, and a little black cat called Buscemi. There, he cooks curries, enjoys beer and quality cinema, and he dreams of a better world.

ALSO AVAILABLE

CHANTECOQ

Chantecoq and the Aubry Affair
Chantecoq and Wilhelm's Spy I: Made In Germany
Chantecoq and Wilhelm's Spy II: The Enemy Within
Chantecoq and Wilhelm's Spy III: The Day of Reckoning
Chantecoq and the Mystery of the Blue Train
Chantecoq and the Haunted House
Chantecoq and the Aviator's Crime
Chantecoq and Zapata
Chantecoq and the Amorous Ogre
Chantecoq and the Père-Lachaise Ghost
Chantecoq and the Condemned Woman
Chantecoq and the Ladykiller
Chantecoq and the Devil's Daughter

By Andrew Lawston

Detective Daintypaws: A Squirrel in Bohemia
Detective Daintypaws: Buscemi at Christmas
Detective Daintypaws: Murder on the Tesco Express
Zip! Zap! Boing!
Voyage of the Space Bastard
Rudy on Rails

Printed in Great Britain
by Amazon